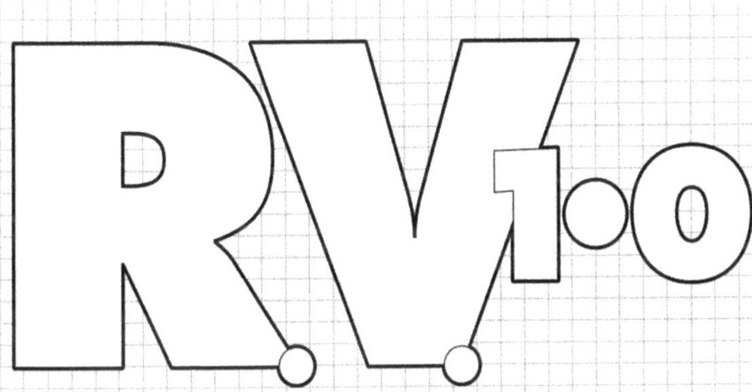

THE BLACK DIAMOND EFFECT® ....Volume 1, No. 52
R.V. 1 • 0

R.V. 1 • 0
© 2025 by Critical Blast Publishing. All Rights Reserved.

Critical Blast Publishing
624 Sunnyhill Drive
Belleville, IL 62223

R.V. 1 • 0
Created & Written, Story, Book Design, Typesetting, Cover Art & Interior Illustrations by George Peter Gatsis.
© 2025 George Peter Gatsis. All Rights Reserved. GeorgePeterGatsis • com

Edited by R.J. Carter.

First Edition Nov 2025

0 9 8 7 6 5 4 3 2 1

ISBN: 978-1-998564-86-6
       Digest

Distributed by Critical Blast Logistics - CriticalBlast.com / PRINTED IN USA.

Road Map

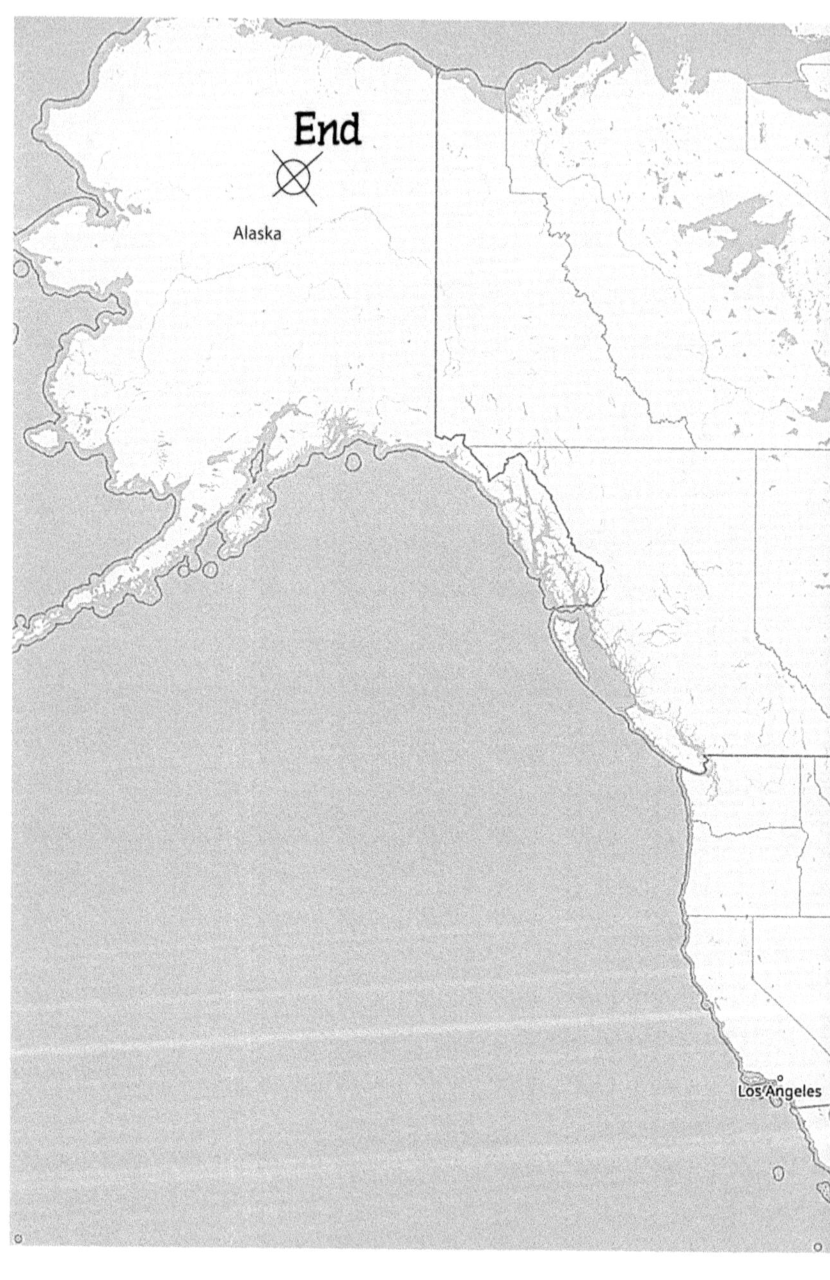

End
Alaska
Los Angeles

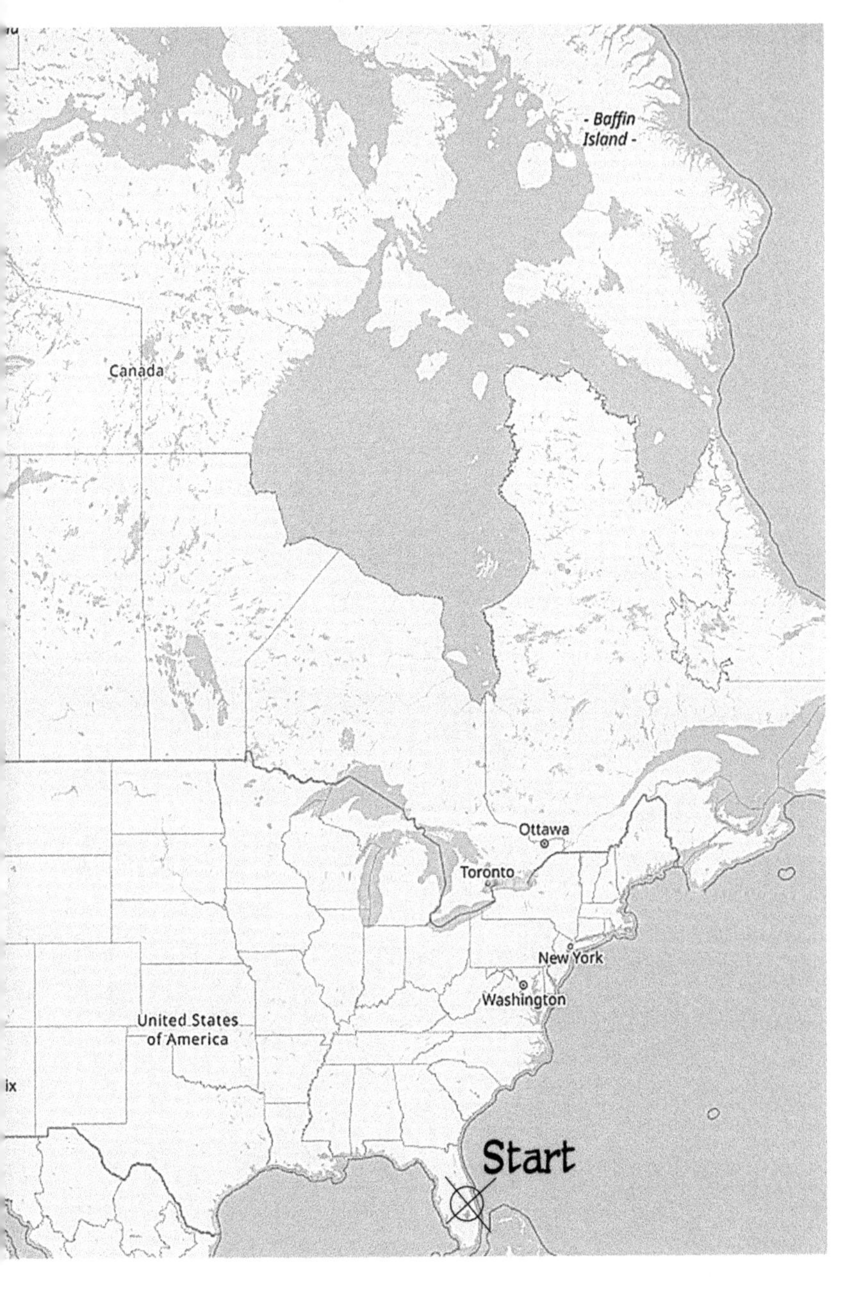

- Baffin Island -
Canada
Ottawa
Toronto
New York
Washington
United States of America
Start

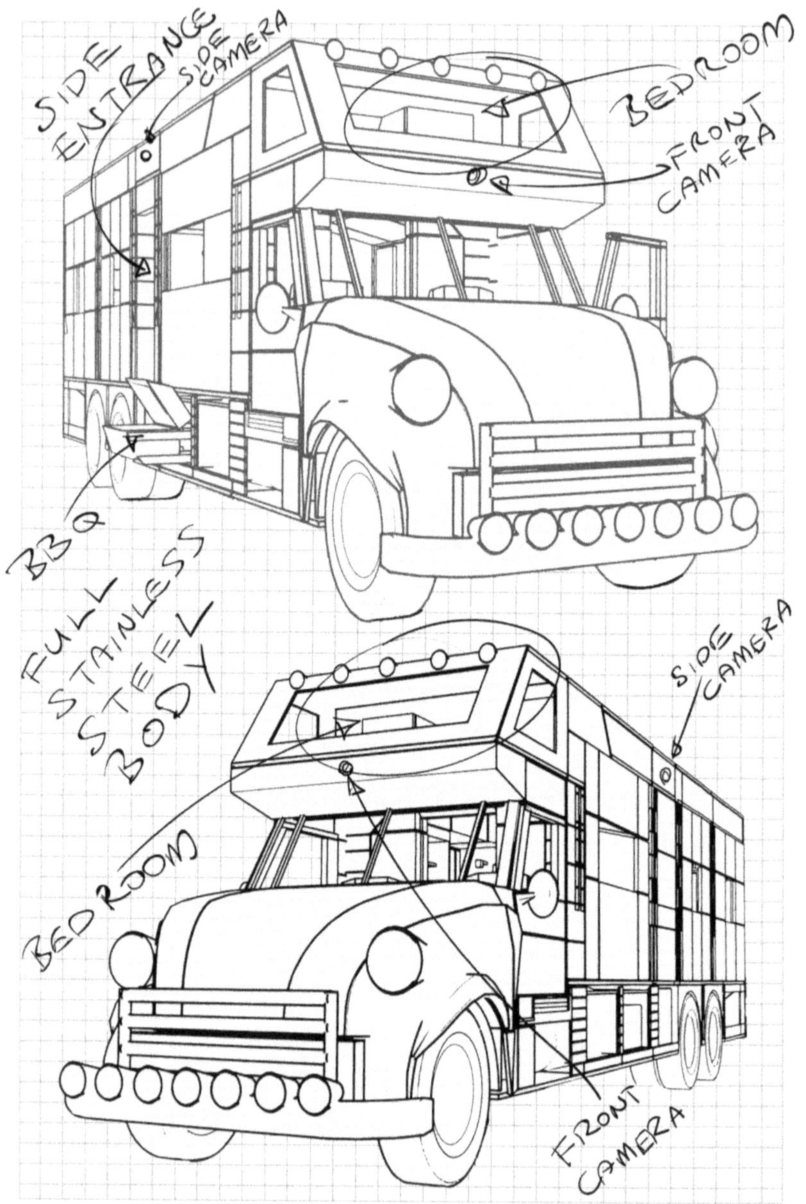

SIDE ENTRANCE
SIDE CAMERA
BEDROOM
FRONT CAMERA
BBQ
FULL STAINLESS STEEL BODY
BEDROOM
SIDE CAMERA
FRONT CAMERA

Chapter 1: Call of the North

The sun hung high above the Atlantic like a sphere of molten gold, its fierce light searing the distant horizon and transforming the restless waves into a vast, undulating sheet of liquid flame. Adam, a thirty-year-old surfer whose hair had been bleached to pale gold by countless days under that same unrelenting sun, and whose skin bore the deep, weathered tan of one who lived in eternal summer, knifed through the foaming crest of a breaker just off Hutchinson Island on Florida's Treasure Coast. His board cut the water with the clean precision of a scalpel, sending up plumes of spray that fanned out behind him like the wings of some aquatic bird in full flight. The ocean was his refuge, the one realm where the clamor of the world dissolved into the eternal cadence of swell and tide. It was midday, the heat bearing down upon the coast like a living weight, and the beach thrummed with the sounds of human vitality—shouts of exhilaration, bursts of laughter, the muffled thud of a volleyball striking sand in the distance.

Hutchinson Island, with its potent surges breaking over shallow reefs, had always been Adam's domain. He had come of age here, mastering the art of the ride at Walton Rocks, where the waves rolled in with dependable rhythm and the shoreline drew a eclectic blend of locals and transient visitors. On this day, the swells rose especially fine, sculpted into flawless peaks by winds blowing from the north and northeast. Adam coaxed the wave to its conclusion, allowing it to propel him nearer to the shore before he leaped lightly from his board, flinging droplets from his sodden hair. His phone, secured within a waterproof pouch lashed to the board, vibrated with persistent demand. He narrowed his eyes against the glare, brushing brine from his lashes as he peered at the screen. Ben calling. Ben, that steadfast companion from high school days, who had forsaken the warmth of sun-drenched sands for the bite of perpetual snow, relocating to Alaska two years prior in pursuit of an ambitious vision: to serve as a military physician while embracing a life detached from the grid of civilization. Adam's lips curved in a grin as he pressed the device to his ear.

"Yo, Ben! What's the word? You turned into a human popsicle yet?" Adam quipped, embedding his board upright in the sand and lowering himself onto a spread towel. The beach pulsed with activity, the ceaseless crash of waves forming an unvarying symphony.

Ben's voice emerged through the line, fractured by static and infused with a pressing urgency. "Adam, I need you. That battered truck of yours—still running?"

Adam chuckled, his gaze drifting to the weathered blue pickup stationed just past the dunes. "She's holding together. What's going on? You sound... off."

"Yeah, the work here's grueling," Ben replied, his tone sinking to a hushed murmur. "I need you to haul something substantial up here. It's a tall order. You ever piloted an RV?"

Adam arched a brow, idly scuffing the sand with his toe. "An RV? You mean one of those rolling domiciles? Nah, I'm a wave-rider, not hauling kids to practice."

Ben offered no mirth in response. "This isn't your standard RV, Adam. It's a bespoke creation. Engineered for the terrain I'm in. I need it brought to a remote speck up here, deep in the Alaskan wilds. Town called Coldfoot. You game?"

Adam reclined, the sun's rays toasting his shoulders with insistent warmth. Alaska. The very name evoked visions of colossal evergreens piercing the sky, razor-edged peaks clawing at the clouds, and air so frigid it could strip the subtropical ease from his bones in an instant. His farthest venture north had been a brief jaunt to Georgia, chasing superior breaks over a mere weekend. Piloting an RV to Alaska struck him as the stuff of delirium, not a simple errand. Yet Ben's voice carried a sharpness, a fusion of pleading and fervor that Adam could not dismiss. They had forged their bond as privates in the service. Ben rarely imposed, but when he did, it invariably signaled matters of gravity.

"What's my cut?" Adam jested, though the hook was already set halfway.

"Adventure," Ben countered. "Plus, you'll have me in your debt. And there's compensation. Sufficient to refurbish that truck, perhaps acquire a fresh board. You collect the RV at Charlie's Chase Coach Mod Shop tomorrow, and I'll handle fuel, meals, all of it. Just deliver it."

Adam gazed seaward, where the waves advanced in their inexorable, mesmerizing rhythm. His existence was uncomplicated—ride the surf, scrape by with sporadic gigs at the beachside stand, bunk at his mother's house, then repeat the cycle. Alaska represented an altogether different entity, an opportunity to shatter the monotony. A flicker ignited within him, one he had not sensed in ages: the stirrings of intrigue.

"Alright, Ben. Count me in. Where's this RV located, exactly?"

Ben released a breath heavy with alleviation. "You're a lifesaver. I'll send the details. A fellow named Charlie. He'll equip you. You'll understand soon enough."

"Okay," Adam affirmed, but the connection had already severed. Moments later, his phone chimed with an incoming message: coordinates, a scheduled hour, and a lone icon—a delicate snowflake.

Adam passed the remainder of the afternoon amid the waves, yet his focus eluded the ocean's embrace. His thoughts wandered northward, to frost-slicked paths and boundless woodlands, to the enigmas enveloping Ben's existence. As the sun descended, bathing the heavens in strokes of amber and rose, restlessness claimed him. He retrieved his board, slung it into the truck's bed, and motored homeward, the briny essence of the sea still adhering to his flesh.

Home manifested as a modest bungalow, shared with his mother, a yoga devotee eternally in quest of her inner equilibrium. The dwelling carried the aromas of smoldering sage and blooming lavender, and his mother was at the counter, whirring a blender into a frothy concoction as he entered.

"Adam! You're radiant," she observed, her tone light and ethereal. "The sea bestowed its gifts today, didn't it?"

"Yeah, Ma," he replied, seizing a glass and filling it with water. "Got a strange ring, though. Ben, way up in Alaska. Wants me to ferry some upscale RV his way."

His mother's eyes gleamed with wonder. "Alaska! Oh, that's a pilgrimage, my dear. The cosmos is summoning you to grandeur. You must heed it."

Adam rolled his eyes yet smiled indulgently. His mother discerned omens in every nuance—a gull's passage heralded transformation, an overcast sky invited contemplation. Perhaps, on this occasion, her intuition held truth. He proceeded to his room, a disordered haven adorned with fading surf imagery on the walls and a mattress laid directly upon the floor. He extracted a duffel from beneath the bed and commenced filling it. T-shirts, denim trousers, a pair of hooded sweatshirts—attire suited to Florida's clime, likely inadequate against Alaskan chill. He added his cherished beanie, green and threadbare at the brim, along with his ancient hiking boots, untouched by earth in years.

As he packed, his mind churned with speculation. What defined this "custom" RV? Why had Ben's demeanor shifted so profoundly? And Coldfoot—what manner of appellation was that for a settlement? He consulted his phone, poring over the scant digital traces. A mere pinpoint on the charts, with a populace scarcely reaching double digits, situated along the Dalton Highway—a thoroughfare that evoked challenge more than convenience. Online fragments spoke of truck halts, dancing auroras, and little beyond. Adam sensed a surge of exhilaration laced with apprehension. This transcended a mere journey; it was a descent into the abyss of the unfamiliar.

He sealed the duffel, his pulse quickening with a blend of anxiety and eagerness. Come morning, he would visit Charlie's establishment and inspect the vessel Ben had ensnared him with. He envisioned himself navigating mountainous expanses, perhaps glimpsing a moose or bear, the RV throbbing beneath him akin to a vessel traversing an oceanic highway of tar. The sea had long been his realm of exploration, but perhaps the hour had arrived for a novel variety of crest.

Dawn's arrival could not hasten sufficiently. Adam bestowed a kiss upon his mother's cheek, claimed his keys, and ventured to his truck, the morning breeze crisp against his skin. The bespoke RV facility lay but a few hours distant, yet it seemed the threshold of another realm. He deposited his bag on the adjacent seat, the engine sputtering awake. As he departed the drive, the daylight appeared more vivid, more keen. Adam stood poised for the odyssey ahead.

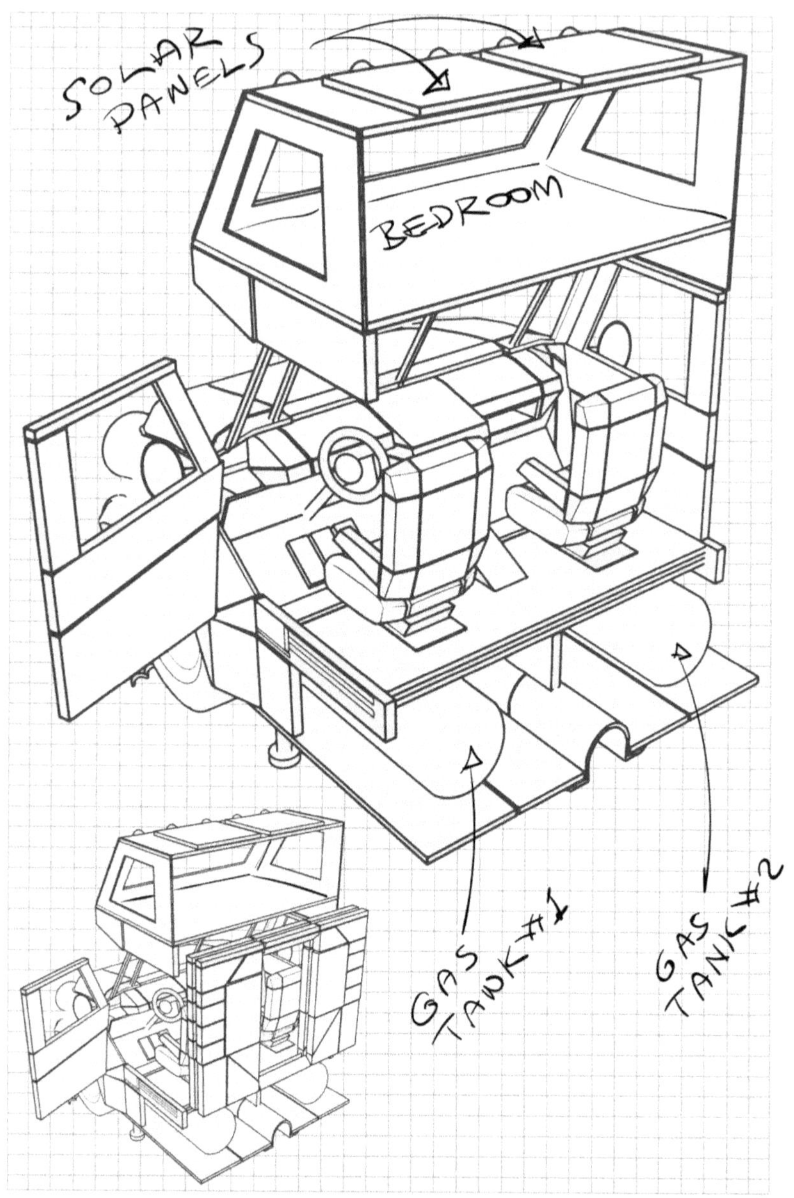

SOLAR PANELS
BEDROOM
GAS TANK #1
GAS TANK #2

Chapter 2: Beast on Wheels

The morning sun was still climbing over the Florida horizon when Adam eased his truck into the lot of Chase Coach, the custom RV shop Ben had pointed him toward. The establishment sprawled like some vast industrial organism, its exterior a mottled expanse of corrugated metal sheets interspersed with weathered signs proclaiming expertise in engine rebuilds and bespoke paint applications. The air thrummed with the sharp clangor of tools and the steady drone of machinery, a vibrant chorus of mechanical endeavor that quickened Adam's pulse with eager expectation. This was no mere repair bay; it was a sanctum of fabrication, where nomadic aspirations were hammered and welded into tangible form.

Slinging his duffel bag across his back, Adam stepped down from his truck, the gravel shifting crunchily beneath his scuffed sneakers. The lot formed a labyrinth of automotive wonders—RVs in every conceivable configuration, bespoke automobiles and compact vans engineered for solitary or duo habitation, plus a handful of eccentric amalgamations that evoked visions of dystopian wastelands. Technicians in oil-smeared coveralls navigated the chaos, some sparking welds, others probing engine innards, a few debating schematics unrolled on an improvised workbench. The tableau pulsed with disorderly vitality, utterly captivating.

A man in his late forties, sporting a salt-and-pepper beard and a name tag declaring "Charlie," caught sight of Adam and beckoned him closer. Charlie's hands bore the rugged calluses of long labor, his gaze keen behind protective eyewear. "You must be Adam," he said, offering a firm handshake. "Ben rang ahead. You're here for the Renegade, right?"

Adam gripped the proffered hand, sensing the coarse grit of Charlie's skin. "Yeah, that's me. This place is wild. What's with all the RVs?"

Charlie's grin flashed with a spark of mischief. "Welcome to the vanguard of mobile existence. We've got it all, from wheeled micro-dwellings to opulent rolling estates. Come on, I'll give you the tour before we reach yours."

They threaded through the workshop, Charlie gesturing toward ongoing creations. One compact RV underwent solar panel integration, destined for a youthful pair embarking on a transcontinental journey. Another was a colossal unit, its hull adorned with a vivid tableau of peaks and waterways, crafted for a sextet of kin. Adam admired the clever adaptations, each vehicle molded precisely to its proprietor's dream. It resembled an exhibition hall, yet the masterpieces here were utilitarian, primed for the open highway.

At last, they halted before a formidable contraption. The heavily modified 2023 Renegade Classic 38CSB stretched forty feet in length, a Super C RV that loomed above its companions. Its shell merged black, silver, and martial gray in sleek harmony, with subtle striations lending it a faintly menacing aura. Ten wheels bore its mass—dual fronts, and quadruple pairs aft, engineered to shoulder the burden of this ambulatory citadel of steel.

"Behold your conveyance," Charlie declared, slapping Adam's shoulder. "She's a beauty, isn't she?"

Adam let out a low whistle, orbiting the RV. It fused opulence with resilience in a way he'd never encountered, the front grille gleaming in polished chrome, windows deeply tinted, and the roof crowned by an enigmatic, angular protrusion that stirred his intrigue. "She's massive," he remarked. "How am I supposed to drive this thing?"

Charlie chuckled. "No sweat, I'll guide you through it. But first, let's inspect the interior."

Charlie stopped, leaned toward Adam, and whispered, "And, don't get me started on the engine. I pulled it from a Racing Horse and wedged it in."

They ascended the entry steps, and Charlie unlocked the door with an antiquated key that seemed better suited to a frontier lockup than modern times. The cabin unveiled a marvel. Mirroring the exterior, floors of stainless steel tiles shimmered beneath diffused recessed illumination, cabinets fashioned from brushed aluminum. Quartz surfaces edged the galley, a dining table stowed flush against the wall amid sumptuous leather benches. The lounge flowed openly, dominated by a sizable flatscreen display pivoted on the bulkhead alongside a capable audio array.

Charlie passed Adam a hefty tome bound in leather, its face embossed with "RV 1•0". "Priority one," he said. "This is the operator's manual. It details the full electrical and plumbing architectures. From solar arrays to the water heater, it's comprehensive. Get acquainted, especially for roadside diagnostics."

Adam leafed through the pages, the illustrations and blueprints attesting to the RV's intricate design. "This is like a textbook," he observed, duly impressed. "Wait a minute! It's all handwritten!"

"Precisely," Charlie confirmed. "Rush order. No time to commission a designer for polished visuals and precise scaling. Now, follow me."

They proceeded aft, and Charlie indicated a floor segment beneath the primary berth. "Observe," he said, depressing a wall-mounted control. The bed elevated smoothly to the overhead, exposing broad floor plates. Charlie toggled a hidden latch on the largest panel and lifted, uncovering a cavernous underfloor bay. "This is a standout bespoke element. All storage, garage, batteries, gasoline generator, waste tanks, potable reservoirs, implements, fuel reservoirs, outdoor grill—everything accessible internally. The garage suits equipment, spare tools, or even a bicycle. Flooring is fortified and hermetically sealed. Should you encounter submersion, this vessel will simply bob along."

Adam leaned into the void, the area unexpectedly ample. "That's insane," he said. "Like having a basement on wheels."

Charlie nodded. "Exactly. Now, let's discuss anchoring."

They returned forward, and Charlie highlighted the tailored stabilizing jacks flanking each axle. "These revolutionize setup," he explained. "In park, engage them to immobilize the RV. They level it superbly, even on irregular ground. Just activate here, and they deploy hydraulically."

Adam observed the demonstration, the jacks descending with a mechanical sigh, elevating the RV fractionally from the surface. "That's… actually really cool," he said. "No more worrying if I forgot the parking brake."

"Precisely, especially if you engage the auxiliary toggle, which deploys augers concealed within the jacks, burrowing deeper for enhanced anchorage." Charlie said. "Safety first."

Next, they approached the command console by the pilot's station. "This is the vigilance array," Charlie elaborated. "Surveillance lenses encircle the RV, viewable from here, the copilot seat, the dining and galley display, or the aft screen. Monitor all aspects—fore, aft, flanks, even the summit. Fully integrated, for constant awareness from within."

Adam nodded, duly impressed. "So, I can watch for polar bears while I'm cooking dinner?"

Charlie laughed. "Or nosy neighbors. It's all about peace of mind."

Finally, they neared a prominent bulkhead panel by the ingress. "This is the distribution matrix," Charlie said. "Central hub for hydraulic and power routing. Toggle between propane, grid, battery, or generator sources as required. Automated primarily, with manual overrides available. The manual elaborates, but it's largely instinctive."

Adam examined the panel, the switches and gauges embodying the RV's adaptability. "This thing's like a pilot's cockpit," he said.

"Close enough," Charlie agreed. "Now, let's check out the roof."

They scaled the slim ladder to the apex, where Charlie indicated the rugged solar collectors yielding 1600 watt-hours and a fortified bivalve enclosure housing the leashed aerial drone. Charlie detailed its operation, the tether serving dual purpose as signal booster and restraint for the robust unit. Adam envisioned it ascending over Alaskan expanses, a vital conduit to civilization.

Back within, Charlie surrendered the keys. "One last thing, no slide outs and she's all yours. She's fueled, fluids verified, and you're cleared. Drive safe, and remember, if you run into trouble, call me." Charlie pauses for a moment and takes out a small paper pouch from his back pocket and hands it to Adam. "Ben told me to give you this. This is your travel money."

Adam nodded, his thoughts accelerating. This wasn't just an RV; it was a declaration, an apparatus forged for exploration. He heaved his duffel onto the copilot perch and settled into the driver's throne, the leather yielding coolly. The instrument cluster sprawled with controls and displays, but Charlie had covered the essentials. He twisted the ignition, and the powerplant thundered awake, a resonant growl reverberating through the cabin.

Easing from the lot, Adam experienced a surge of thrill tempered by apprehension. The RV maneuvered distinctly from his truck, its mass an ever-present factor.

That's when it hit him. Adam stopped, jumped out and rushed to his truck that he was leaving behind. He grabs his surf board and stores it away in the RV's garage. Charlie couldn't help but laugh and shout, "Good luck, kid!"

Adam hopped back into the RV's driver seat, the sun glinting off the chrome, he couldn't help but smile. Alaska was calling, and he was answering, with a beast on wheels, ready to conquer the unknown. He turned on the radio and randomly picked a station to listen. All that was coming through the speakers was static. "Oh well," Adam smiled. "Almost perfect," as he drove away.

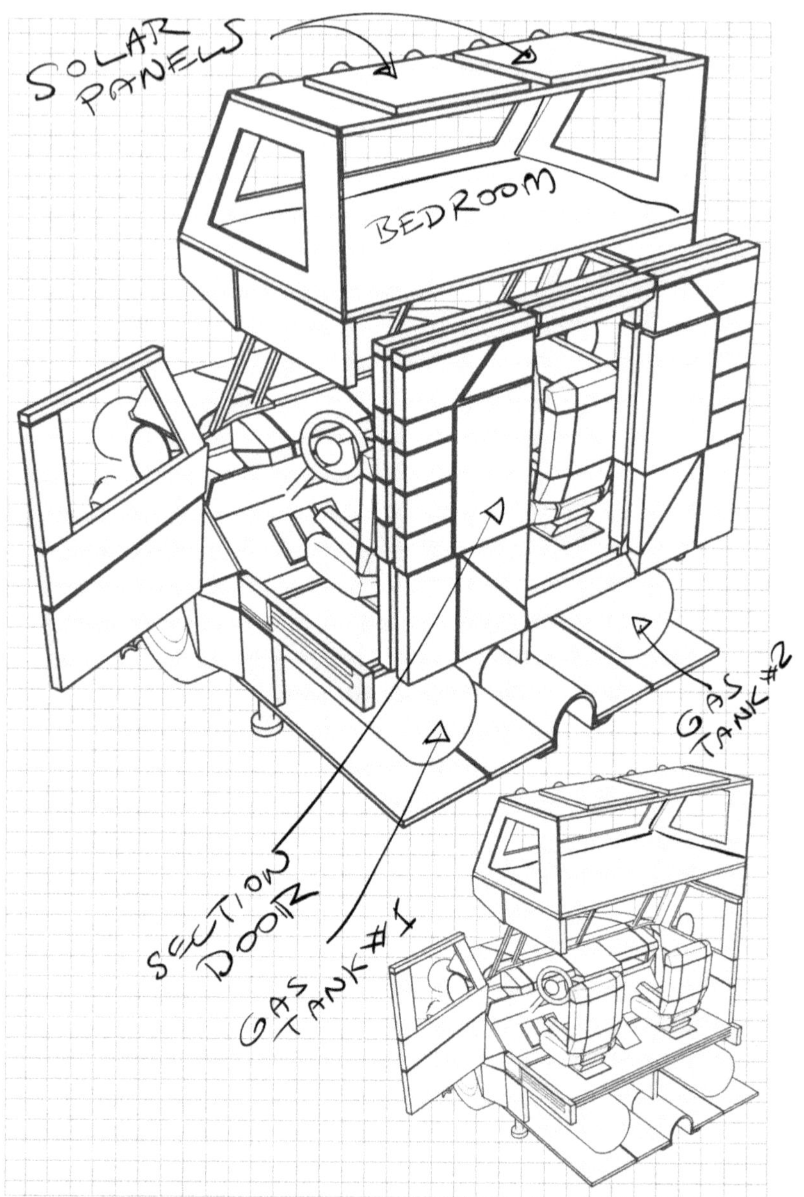

SOLAR PANELS
BEDROOM
SECTION DOOR
GAS TANK #1
GAS TANK #2

Chapter 3: Storm's Edge

Adam eased the RV into the gas station just off the highway, where the rain slashed down in relentless curtains. The sky hung low and sullen, a vast expanse of brooding gray, while thunder growled far off like some ancient beast stirring in its sleep. He guided the hulking vehicle to the pumps, tires hissing through deepening puddles, and set about filling the tank. The station itself was a humble outpost, a lone island of pumps beneath a dented metal canopy, linked to a variety store that squatted nearby. The sign overhead proclaimed "Ray's Fuel & Supplies" in faded letters, the paint flaking away, yet the lights inside burned steady and defiant.

As Adam worked the pump, his gaze drifted to the station owner, Ray—a lean, wiry figure in his late forties, his face etched deep by years of sun and wind—and his two sons, Tyler at sixteen and Liam at fourteen, all of them laboring over the storm doors that served as the store's primary bulwark. Those doors were formidable things, heavy metal frames built to defy the fury of tempests, but rust had gnawed at the hinges, and one sagged drunkenly at an odd angle. Ray perched on a ladder, screwdriver gripped tight, while Tyler braced the door with steady hands, and Liam passed up tools from an open box on the wet ground. Rain plastered their clothes to their skins, yet they pressed on with the grim resolve of those who knew survival demanded no less.

Within the store, a cluster of folk had gathered—families with wide-eyed children, adults of every age—huddled in tense silence, peering out through the barred windows at the repairs. The air inside thrummed with unease, heavy with the scent of damp concrete and the sharp, electric tang of approaching lightning. Adam took it all in with a quick sweep: the worried faces, the little ones clinging to threadbare stuffed toys or their parents' fingers.

With the tank full, the wind suddenly surged, whipping up to the raw power of a Category 5 hurricane, clawing at the world with invisible talons. It seized the unfastened storm doors and wrenched them free in a thunderous crash of metal, twisting the frames like scrap as they tore away. Ray and his boys, hands linked in a desperate chain, lurched back into the store just in time, tumbling through the entrance as the gale swallowed the building whole. The variety store teetered on the brink, winds howling through the gaping front like a predator's maw, threatening to peel the roof away in shreds.

Adam felt the moment's peril like a jolt and ducked into the RV for cover. Through the windshield, he saw the store's roof lifting, the whole structure moaning in protest against the onslaught. No time for second thoughts—he fired up the engine, the diesel's deep roar cutting through the chaos. He gunned it forward, crashing the RV's cab through the front doors, wedging it tight to form a barrier that sealed out the wind's grasping fingers and spared the roof from ruin. Those inside stared, eyes bulging in the dim light, as the RV's jacks whirred into action, boring down into the concrete with mechanical precision. The hydraulic scream filled the space, locking the vehicle in place like an anchor in a raging sea.

Adam stepped out then, strolling to the cash register as if the storm were mere background noise. He plucked a handful of beef jerky packs from the shelf, the wrappers crackling softly in his grasp, and set them by the till. His eyes found Ray close by, the man's expression a tangle of gratitude and stunned wonder. "What do I owe for the gas?" Adam asked, voice steady amid the bedlam.

Ray gaped at him, then at the RV, where the jacks had just fallen silent. "You… you saved our hides," he rasped, throat raw. "Jerky's free. Gas too. Take anything you want, friend."

Adam gave a faint nod, a ghost of a smile touching his lips. "Thanks, Ray. Here's hoping it holds."

Beyond the walls, hail erupted, chunks the size of golf balls hammering the RV's shell like artillery. Lightning strobed, casting everything in harsh, fleeting white. Inside, murmurs of thanks rippled through the crowd, the children gazing in open-mouthed wonder. Tyler and Liam, breaths still heaving, watched the RV's bulk steady the building. The storm doors lay mangled and forgotten on the lot, but the vehicle stood as their salvation.

Ray, practical to the core, turned to his sons. "Come on, boys—let's shore up what we can. Tyler, fetch the plywood from the back. Liam, give me a hand with the windows." The lads nodded sharply, moving with practiced speed. Ray had weathered gales before, but this one dwarfed them all. The RV's timely arrival was nothing short of miraculous, and he knew it deep in his bones.

The storm howled on, and Adam monitored the RV's gauges: exterior temps soaring, batteries draining fast, yet the systems endured. The air filters labored, barring the hail and rain's intrusion. Radio spat nothing but static, phone dead as ever. He leaned against the counter, jerky in hand, observing Ray and the boys at their tasks—a tableau of human grit, a family forging unity against the wild.

At last, the fury ebbed, hail dwindling to patters, winds easing to sighs. Adam slipped back into the RV via the driver's door, emerged through the side one by the kitchen, and tapped switches on the midway panel at the stairs' base. The jacks retracted with a pneumatic hiss. The station bore scars—the doors vanished—but the store endured. Ray descended the steps and approached, hand outstretched. "Thank you," he said, voice thick. "You're a goddamn hero."

Adam clasped it, jerky still clutched in his free hand. "Just passing through," he replied, though his eyes hinted at deeper currents. He climbed aboard, engine rumbling awake, and eased out, leaving the door frame dinged but mendable with some honest work.

All within the variety store watched the RV vanish down the road's uncertain bend.

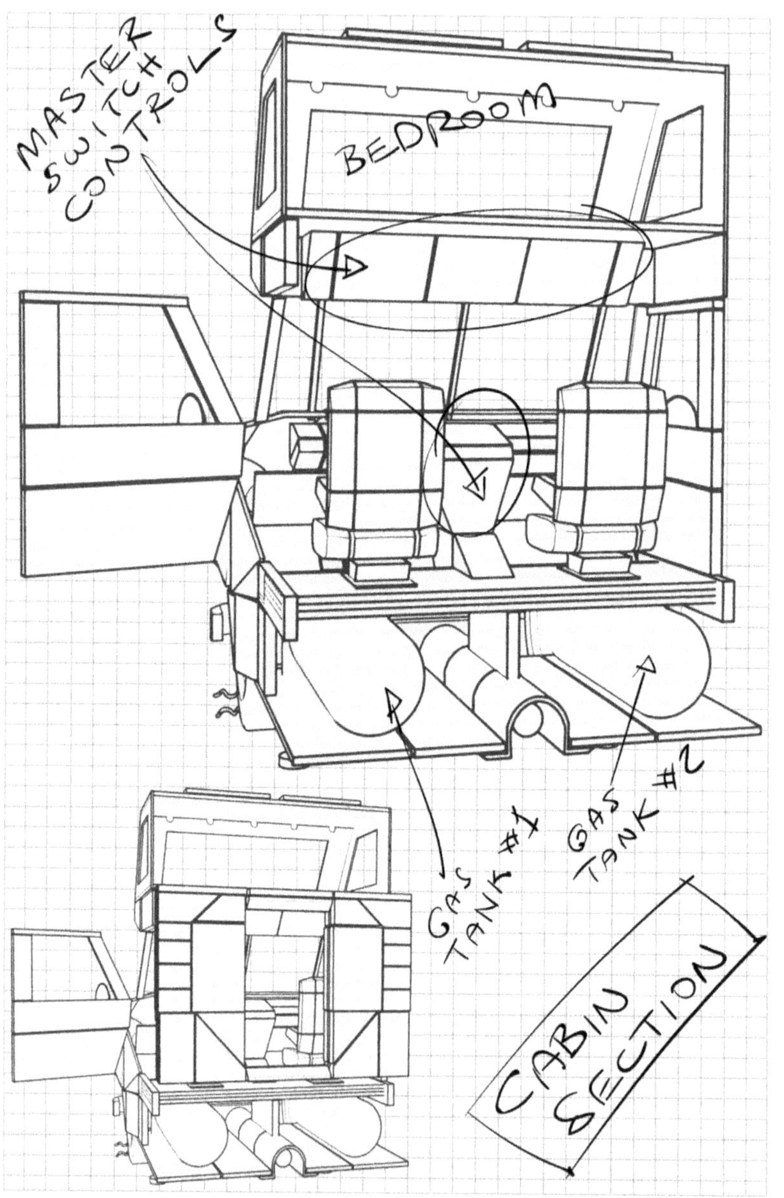

MASTER SWITCH CONTROLS
BEDROOM
GAS TANK #1
GAS TANK #2
CABIN SECTION

Chapter 4: Wrath of the Plains

Adam eased the RV along the highway, the blacktop unspooling like a ribbon across the vast, unyielding flatness of the land. Overhead, the sky burned a fierce, unblemished blue, the sun hammering down on the pavement with relentless force, yet the atmosphere carried an odd, oppressive weight, a subtle itch that crawled along the nape of his neck. Vehicles—cars, pickups, even a scattering of big rigs—hurtled past in the oncoming lanes, their drivers' faces reduced to fleeting smears of haste and alarm. Adam spared them scarcely a thought; his itinerary demanded adherence.

As he maintained his steady pace, four rugged Humvees, bristling with modifications, thundered by on his right, churning up plumes of dust from the barren shoulder. Storm chasers, no doubt, their rigs festooned with whip antennas, dome cameras, and an array of instruments that fairly shouted their pursuit of atmospheric fury. Adam caught a glimpse of them in the rearview mirror, their taillights dwindling into the haze. "Something sizable brewing ahead," he murmured under his breath, redirecting his focus to the endless stretch before him.

He twisted the radio knob from the satellite feed's melodic drone to a local broadcast, the tuner hissing with interference until it locked in. The broadcaster's tone was edged with immediacy, slicing through the crackle. "This is a Particularly Dangerous Situation (PDS) Tornado Warning for portions of central Oklahoma, encompassing Oklahoma City. Multiple tornadoes are confirmed on the ground, with the strongest projected to parallel the Interstate. Take shelter without delay if you lie in its path."

Adam's pulse stuttered. He glanced at his phone—dead, no bars. Snatching a folded road map from the passenger seat, its edges frayed from handling, he spread it across the wheel, steering with one hand while tracing with the other. The bold red marker trail he'd inked slashed diagonally across the nation, and a swift orientation placed him squarely amid the alerted sector, his route crossing the peril like a fatal intersection. The insight struck with visceral force. Traffic from the northbound lanes had vanished entirely; only he remained, with those Humvees now mere specks on the distant horizon.

The breeze escalated into gusts, the heavens dimming as though a cosmic dimmer had been engaged. Adam scanned left—endless prairie, unbroken. The mirror revealed vacancy behind. Then to the right, and a chill seized his veins. A colossal vortex churned toward him, its funnel a brooding, turbulent column etched against the slate-gray vault.

He stomped the brake, the RV fishtailing to a halt with a shriek of rubber on asphalt. The wind's assault commenced in earnest, buffeting the vehicle like a vessel in gale-tossed seas. Adam strained for the glove box, the seat belt restraining him; with a sharp click, he released it and dove forward, seizing the owner's manual. Pages fluttered in the tumult as he located the emergency protocols—stabilization procedures. The RV bucked wildly now, a carnival ride unleashed by nature's caprice, blasts hammering from every quarter.

His fingers danced over the controls, activating the leveling jacks; hydraulics whirred to life with a mechanical keen. The rig lurched sideways, drawn inexorably toward the maelstrom, the steel legs gouging furrows in the roadway. Dashboard lights shifted from crimson warning to verdant readiness, confirming deployment. He triggered the anchors next, and a rhythmic drilling echoed through the cabin as augers bit into the concrete.

The violence peaked; Adam tumbled from the captain's chair, impacting the floor with a jarring thud. For an instant, the entire chassis lifted, jacks groaning in protest against the uplift. Then it crashed earthward, the shudder fading to a persistent quiver. The tornado enveloped him utterly, its bellow a primordial thunder, the exterior a whirlwind of hurtling fragments.

Hauling himself upright, Adam secured the nearest couch harness, the buckle snapping home with finality. Through the window, he beheld a macabre ballet: shards of structures, uprooted flora, even livestock pinwheeling in the chaos. Minutes dragged like hours under the onslaught, until, with abrupt mercy, the fury receded. Light pierced the gloom anew, the sun reclaiming its dominion, and the funnel retreated into the distance, a shrinking specter.

Adam sagged against the cushions, the surge of endorphins receding. A laugh escaped him, raw and cathartic. "Quite the initiation into Tornado Alley," he declared, the utterance laced with equal parts deliverance and astonishment.

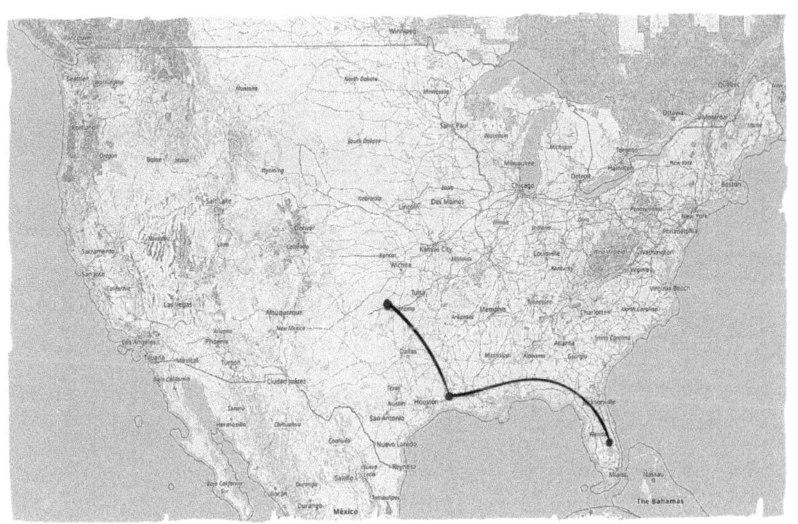

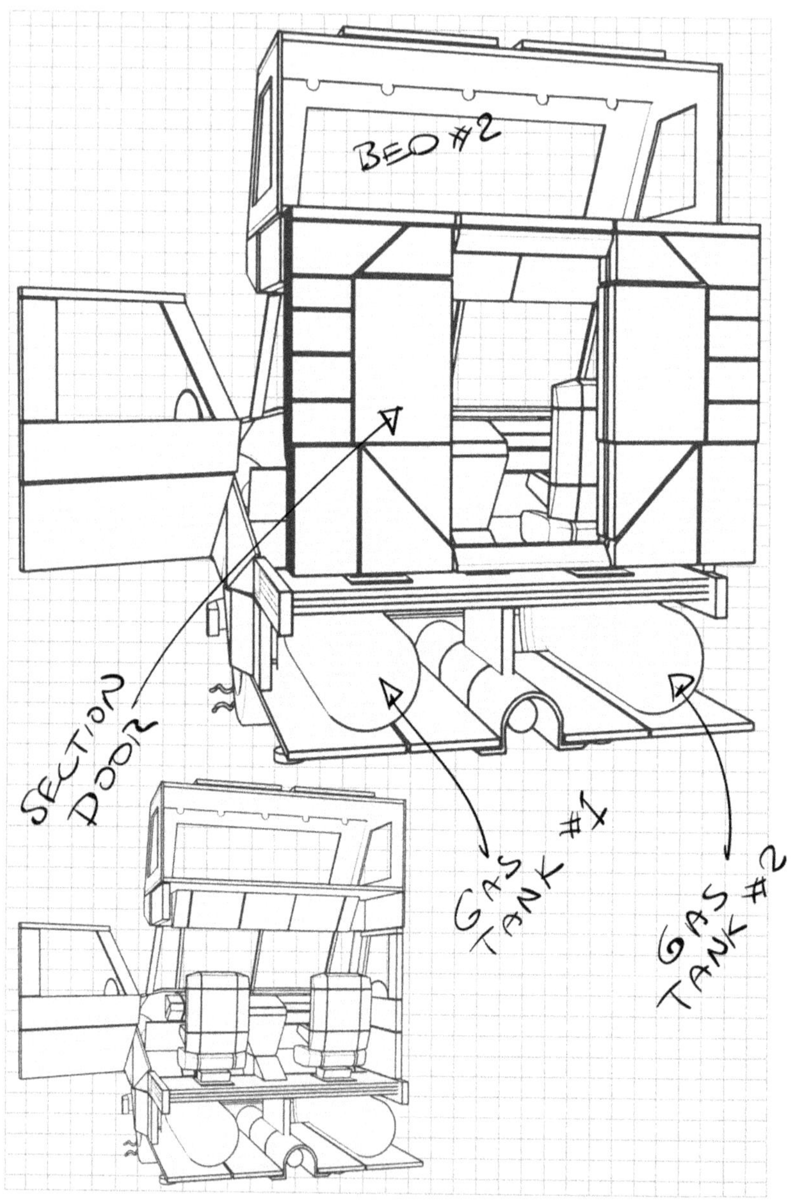
BED #2
SECTION DOOR
GAS TANK #1
GAS TANK #2

Chapter 5: Desert's Breath

Adam piloted the lumbering RV across the sun-blasted reaches of New Mexico's Chihuahuan Desert, where the land unfurled in an unbroken sweep of arid immensity. The heavens arched overhead in flawless azure, the sun a pitiless furnace suspended in the void, while the atmosphere hung parched and brittle, stirred now by a rising gust that whispered of ancient, unforgiving forces. The vehicle thrummed steadily along the ribbon of highway, the terrain a vast ocean of sagebrush and drifting sands that seemed to breathe with a life of its own. He cast a glance at the map spread beside him, its crimson line tracing their diagonal traverse across the continent like a vein of blood in the earth's skin. "We're holding pace," he murmured to the empty cab, "yet those earlier snags are gnawing at the margins."

Scarcely had the thought settled when his gaze snagged on a van marooned beside the thoroughfare, canted awkwardly into a gulch as if the desert itself had reached up to claim it. A lone figure stood adjacent, hands planted firmly on hips, her expression a tapestry woven of exasperation and weary surrender. Adam eased the RV to a halt, its tires grinding protestingly over the gravel verge. "Trouble ahead," he declared to the windshield, drawing the beast to rest.

Emerging into the open, he was assaulted by a palpable barrier of heat, as though the air had thickened into a tangible shroud. The woman—mid-thirties, her short blonde locks tousled by the wind, clad in a jacket filmed with the desert's fine grit—raised a hand in greeting. "Grateful you paused," she called, her words slicing through the mounting breeze. "Name's Ester. Van's mired fast; no budging it."

Adam inclined his head, surveying the predicament with a practiced eye. The vehicle listed precariously, one wheel dangling in empty air above a trench that yawned like a hungry maw. "Adam here. Summoned aid?"

Ester's denial came with a shake of her head. "Phone shattered in the mishap. No contacts etched in memory. Can't raise my companions."

Adam's brow creased. "Companions? Their whereabouts?"

Her gesture swept broadly toward the western horizon. "Buried in the desert's heart. I served as the supply runner for a cadre of scientists. They're out there, capturing the cosmos on film, trying to prove the Earth is a lot bigger than we're lead to believe. I bore sustenance, power cells, garments, fuel—the vitals."

Adam weighed the perils in silence. The journey's prior hitches had eroded his buffer; a traverse through this wasteland might reclaim lost hours. "Distance?"

"Roughly fifty miles yonder," Ester replied, her arm arcing in emphasis. "Encamped with scopes and lenses. Bereft of practical cunning, though—pure scholars."

He initiated a call for roadside succor, the device crackling with erratic interference—a persistent curse since the odyssey's dawn, signals fracturing like mirages in the heat. Why this perpetual betrayal? he pondered as the dispatcher's voice emerged faint and fractured. "Dispatch ETA: one full day. You're adrift in isolation."

Terminating the link, Adam turned to Ester. "A day? Unacceptable. Your cohort won't endure sans provisions." He unfurled the map anew; she indicated a remote speck amid the dunes. "Thereabouts."

Contemplation yielded decision. "Very well," he stated. "We'll ferry those goods to them. But we carve straight through the wilds."

Ester's gaze flared. "Certain? The terrain's a beast."

Adam's smile flashed like a blade. "This rig's forged for such trials."

They transferred the cargo into the RV's rear hold, Adam vigilant lest his surfboard suffer abrasion. Methodically, they hefted cartons of edibles, containers of energy stores, sacks of apparel, and canisters of petrol. Ester recounted the prelude: "Convoy formation. Lead jeep, mid-van laden with instruments, pressed onward. I lingered at the final outpost to mend an oil seep. Meant to trail with essentials. Then this chasm... as if the sands conspired to engulf me."

With the haul secured, Adam resumed the pavement briefly before diverging into the trackless expanse, guided by the compass's unerring needle. Ester availed herself of the lavatory's amenities, consumed a nutrient slab, and reclined upon the sofa, the RV's cooled confines a bastion against the exterior inferno.

Hours slipped by in rhythmic monotony until, on the shimmering horizon, a cluster materialized—their conveyances catching the solar glare like distant beacons. Yet peril loomed: a colossal sandstorm barreled forth, a towering rampart of ochre and umber, devouring the landscape in its advance. Ester vaulted to the copilot's perch, complexion ashen. "That's the lot. But they'll perish in that maelstrom—grown fledglings, devoid of survival's edge."

Adam depressed the accelerator, the engine bellowing defiance. "Brace yourselves."

At the stargazing enclave, Ester's associates—Dr. Elena Marquez, astrophysicist of forty years; Dr. Samuel Lee, planetary savant aged thirty-five; and the nascent scholars Maya Patel, twenty-eight, and Carlos Rodriguez, twenty-six—labored frantically to stow their optical arrays. Resting cocoons were stashed within the van, a vain bulwark against the abrasive tide. The uncovered jeep already succumbed, half-interred in shifting grains.

The storm's vanguard lashed flesh and metal alike with stinging fury. Adam's RV surged in, slewing to a halt amid a plume of dust. Ester burst from the portal, voice piercing the gale: "Into the RV—now!"

The tempest's full fury descended as Carlos, encumbered by imaging gear, stumbled aboard last. The hatch sealed with finality; Adam engaged the fortification protocol, deploying armored shutters over lateral and aft vistas. Solely the forward panes afforded sight, exterior sensors rendered blind by the swirling chaos.

The vehicle shuddered in the onslaught's grip. Adam deployed the stabilizers, hydraulics sighing as they bit into the unstable substrate. Adjacent automobiles vanished into the ochre veil. Swiveling his command seat, Adam eased back as Ester and her circle exhaled in collective relief.

"Appears we're entrenched for the duration," Adam observed. "Anyone famished?"

Ester interjected: "Provisions lie in the external bay—venturing forth would flay us alive in that scourge."

Adam traversed the aisle to the sleeping quarters, triggered the concealed mechanism; the berth ascended and nested against the overhead, unveiling an access hatch. He unlatched it, granting overhead entry to the crammed stowage. Ester distributed the parcels to her comrades.

Adam noted: "Aquifers brim full—facilities, potable reserves, and galley all operational."

Dr. Elena inquired: "External communion feasible?"

Adam assayed, yielding only discord. "Extending the aerial drone would invite its annihilation in the gales."

He added wryly: "Farewell to our abbreviated route," as pebbles hammered the windscreen and hull in erratic tattoo.

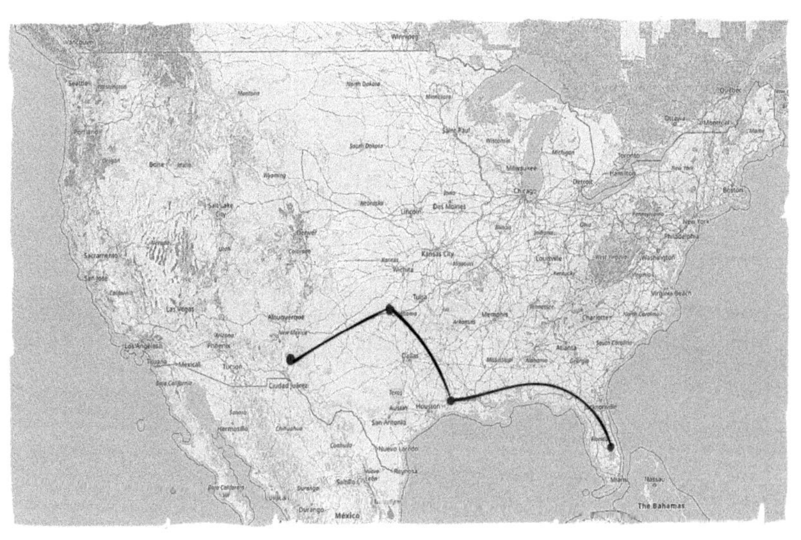

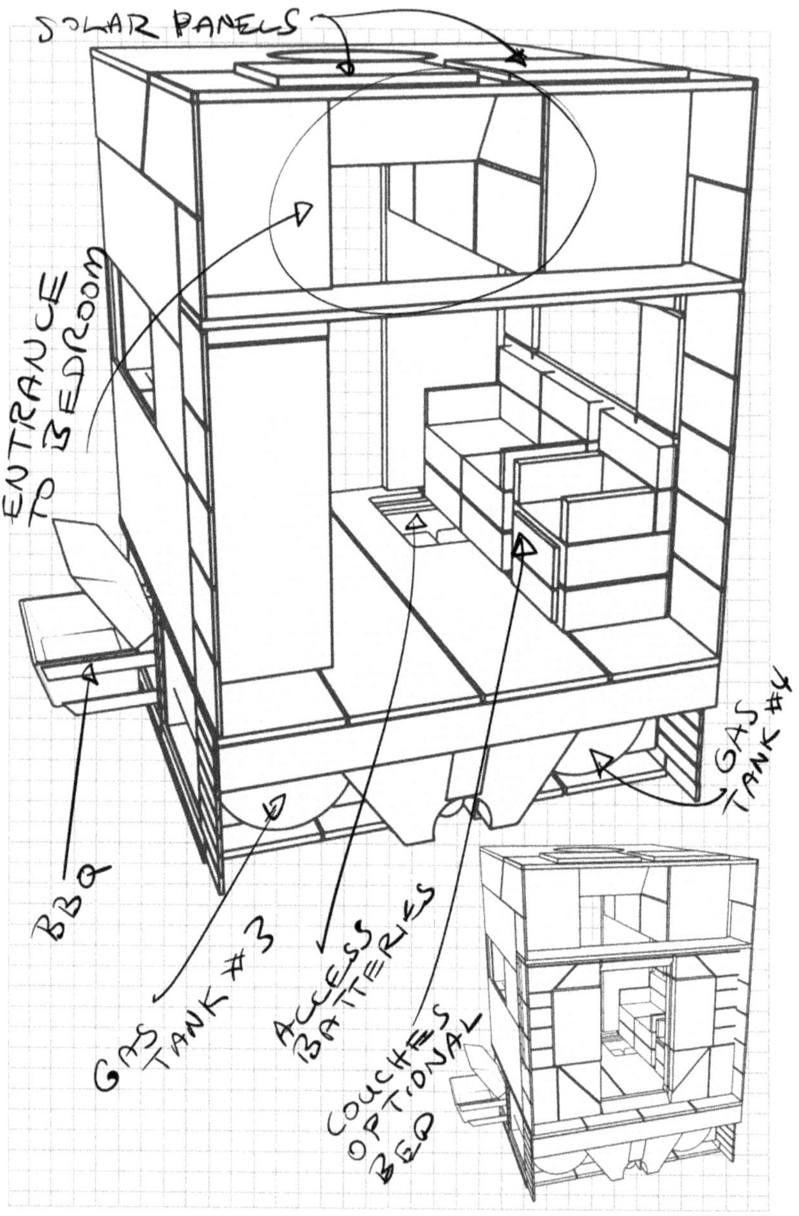

SOLAR PANELS
ENTRANCE TO BEDROOM
BBQ
GAS TANK #3
ACCESS BATTERIES
COUCHES OPTIONAL BED
GAS TANK #4

Chapter 6: Flood and the Fugitives

Adam eased the RV onto the gravel shoulder of that desolate highway, where the bone-dry riverbed mocked the black-bellied clouds gathering far upstream. The sky itself was a merciless azure, the sun a white-hot coin hammering down on the parched earth, yet the air carried a weight, an electric hush that crawled along his skin like invisible insects. He climbed out, boots crunching on sun-baked grit, and drank in the savage splendor of it all—the crimson rock spires thrusting skyward, the thorny scrub clinging to life in defiance of the desert's indifference. So different from Florida's salt-kissed shores and swaying palms. Behind him, the RV idled with a low, contented thrum, its solar arrays winking like polished scales in the glare, the drone antenna folded neat and tight atop the roof. He had Ben on the line, voices bridging the miles as they hashed over the road already devoured.

"Man, this thing's a beast," Adam said, propping himself against the RV's flank, feeling the faint vibration of its heart through the metal. "Handled the tornado like it was nothing."

Ben's reply came back with that easy assurance, crackling faintly over the connection. "Told you. It's built for anything. You're just scratching the surface."

Adam chuckled, scuffing at the dust with his boot. "Yeah, well, I'm about to scratch some more. Headed to the next checkpoint, then up the coast. You sure this thing can handle Alaska?"

"Trust me," Ben said. "I designed it for the extreme weather up here."

Before Adam could fire back, a guttural roar split the sky—not thunder, but the radio inside the RV erupting in urgent tones. "This is a Flash Flood Warning. Seek higher ground immediately. Heavy rainfall upstream has caused a surge heading your way." And then, as if the desert itself conspired against them, a sleek private aircraft—a rejiggered Boeing 727-200, ferrying ten prisoners under U.S. Marshal escort—dropped from the heavens onto the highway's cracked spine. Tires screamed against asphalt in a shriek that set teeth on edge, the pilot compelled earthward by a thunderstorm's fury, lightning forking like vengeful spears that rendered the air unsafe for wings. Engines coughed and sputtered, the pilot's voice sputtering over open channels: "Emergency landing due to thunderstorm."

Aboard, the three prisoners sat shackled at wrist and ankle, yet unbound to their seats by the iron dictates of FAA rules. The four Marshals, drilled in the rituals of aerial crises, found their poise shattered by the abrupt descent.

Prisoner Marcus, once a soldier with eyes sharpened by battle's edge, spotted the flicker of uncertainty in the guards. He leaned close to Lena, the silver-tongued deceiver whose words could bend minds like reeds, and Diego, the jittery pilferer driven by raw need. "Now's our chance." They occupied the rear rows, their restraints fitted with just enough slack to invite fate.

The flood warning howled outside, underscored by the mounting thunder of water on the move. The Marshals scrambled to anchor the plane and summon aid from the ground, their focus splintered like fractured glass. Marcus palmed a hidden sliver of metal—a lock pick secreted in his shoe's sole—and worked it with practiced finesse until his wrists came free. Lena feigned a swoon, crumpling dramatically to pull one Marshal's gaze astray. Diego, hands quaking yet resolute, mirrored the act, liberating himself in heartbeats and snatching the Marshals' sidearms in a frantic sweep.

Marcus drove his boot into the emergency exit window; glass exploded outward in a glittering cascade. The Marshals bellowed, "Stop!" but the pandemonium of touchdown, the siren's wail, and the breakout's lightning strike drowned their commands. Marcus, Lena, and Diego wriggled through the jagged maw, edges slicing orange fabric yet sparing flesh, and tumbled to the scorching highway. The pavement seared through their flimsy soles like brands. Diego pressed a pistol into each of their hands.

The floodwaters crested the horizon now, a churning murof mud and debris barreling down the riverbed. The escapees bolted, their garish jumpsuits blazing like signal fires against the ocher waste, pulses hammering with the wild surge of freedom. They had moments, perhaps less, before order reasserted itself. Ahead loomed the RV, a hulking sanctuary on wheels.

Adam dove back inside, the door sealing with a pneumatic sigh, phone clamped to his ear, as the trio staggered across the asphalt in search of shadow. "Get out of the car!" Marcus thundered, his command riding the crescendo of approaching doom.

Gunfire cracked the air then, a staccato storm between Marshals and fugitives, the RV ensnared in the deadly crossfire. Rounds spanged off its hide with the sharp ring of hail on tin. Adam crouched low, blood thundering in his ears, while Ben's voice cut through: "Adam, you okay? Sounds like trouble."

"Yeah, trouble's an understatement," Adam muttered, risking a glance through the window. Tires sagged with a hiss, pierced by errant lead, and the dashboard chimed in alarm. "Tire pressure critical."

Ben's tone stayed level, a rock in the torrent. "Don't panic. The tires are self-healing. The exterior and windows are bulletproof too. You're safe in there. Now, check the tire pressure indicators on the dashboard. See the red lights? Flick the manual switches for those specific tires. The system will inject a coagulating gas, seal the punctures, and re-inflate them."

Adam obeyed, fingers dancing over the controls as crimson warnings pulsed. Switches flipped; a soft hiss permeated the cabin, tires knitting themselves whole, pressure climbing back to green. "Holy smokes," he breathed. "This thing's incredible!"

"And don't get a scratch on it," Ben warned.

Adam forced a laugh amid the bedlam. "Sorry buddy, gonna have to go back to the shop and buff it all off."

The waters loomed nearer, a frothing barricade devouring the riverbed. Adam mashed the accelerator; the RV's engine bellowed awake, surging forward. The prisoners, seeing their shield vanish, turned their fire on the fleeing fortress—bullets glancing away like rain on stone. Exposed now, Marcus let his weapon fall, Lena spat an oath, and Diego thrust his hands skyward. The Marshals closed in, irons flashing as they reclaimed their charges. Adam powered onward, the peril shrinking in the mirrors.

"Nice work on the modifications," he said into the phone. "You're welcome," Ben replied, static gnawing at the words. "Just remember-" The line died with a pop.

Adam pressed on, the flood receding astern, the RV growling its defiance along the highway. Self-mending tires, an impervious shell, windows that mocked gunfire—it was a rolling citadel, revelation in motion. He eyed the steady gauges, a grin tugging at his lips. Whatever the road hurled next, let it come.

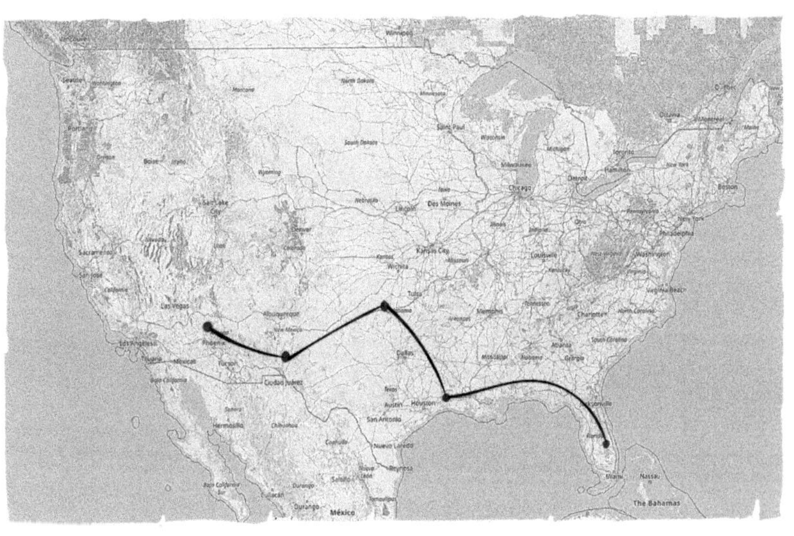

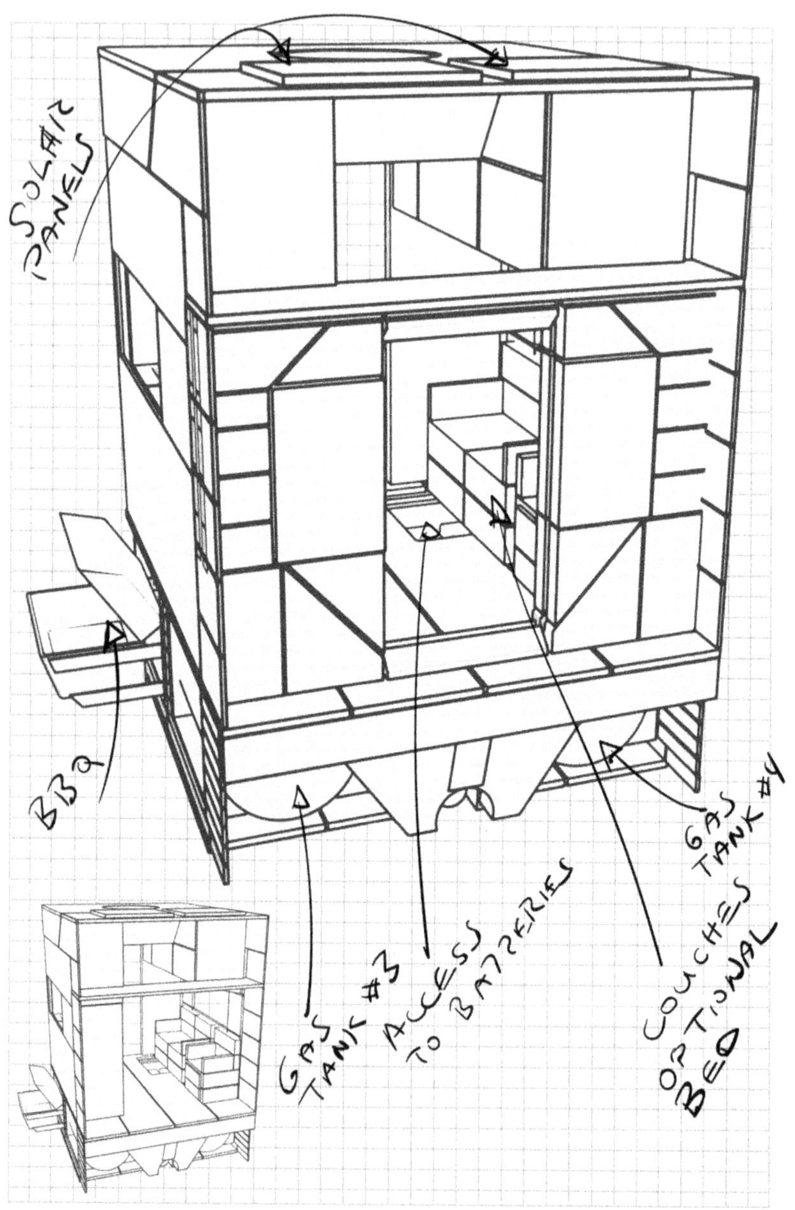

SOLAR PANELS
BBQ
GAS TANK #3
ACCESS TO BATTERIES
COUCHES OPTIONAL BED
GAS TANK #4

Chapter 7: Lava's Embrace

Adam guided the RV across the sun-blasted desert, its engines purring with the steady contentment of well-tuned machinery. The highway had fallen away hours ago. Ben's voice crackled from the phone speaker, half-drowned in static, "Adam, hello?"

He shook his head to the empty cab, the landscape outside blurring into a haze of ocher and gold. "Ben, the connection sucks. Try calling back!"

As the desert's fringe drew near, the highway appeared ahead like a dark ribbon unspooled across the arid expanse, promising the relative ease of paved travel en route to Alaska. Yet something snagged his attention—a haphazard gathering of vehicles and figures, thin plumes of smoke ascending, the unmistakable aroma of charred meat drifting on the dry, heated breeze. All of it poised above fissures where molten lava glowed with malevolent patience.

He eased the RV to a halt beside the tableau, positioning it securely on firm, verdant terrain at the highway's verge. Stepping out, he felt the heat slam against him like a living force, and surveyed the disorder. Automobiles sat abandoned in erratic patterns, makeshift spits rotating lazily over the lava cracks, while a considerable number of inebriated souls wandered in aimless patterns. A youthful hillbilly named Frankie—perhaps twenty, sporting a scruffy beard and a cap frayed at the edges—jogged up to him. "Hey, mister, you got a chain and winch for your RV?"

Adam inspected the RV's storage compartment, largely vacated after disgorging the scientists' gear. "Let me see," he replied, circling the vehicle. He swung open the passenger door, delved into the glove box, and extracted the hand-scrawled manual. Paging through it, he located the entry: "Yes, there's a chain and winch system under the back of the RV. Unlatch the spare tire, swing it to one side, and it exposes the chain, winch, and levers for neutral, lock, and retract. Powered by the gas generator for torque."

"What do you need it for?" Adam inquired.

Frankie gestured toward the lava. "I think this place is gonna blow. Can't convince my drunk friends to leave without the food."

Adam waved off the notion. "It's just minor volcanic activity. No signs of a big eruption. You're safe for now." But then the earth grumbled in protest, and several spits toppled, their contents flash-cooked to perfection in the searing flow.

He shifted the winch to neutral, and Frankie seized the hooked terminus, sprinting toward his companions. The ground shuddered anew, and a pair of automobiles vanished into the widening crevices. Now all twelve hillbillies were in full panic as Frankie arrived among them, fastening the chain to a red convertible. "Get on the car!" he shouted, the terrain fracturing further beneath them.

The hillbillies—a varied assemblage of men and women ranging from their twenties to fifties—clutched their moonshine jugs and beer bottles, clambering aboard the vehicle while Frankie signaled to Adam. Adam engaged the retract lever, but the convertible's mass proved excessive, and the RV began inching perilously toward the lava field.

The car halted briefly, lava licking at its undercarriage. A voice cried out, "The gas tank's gonna blow!" Another, thick with slur, countered, "Nah, we emptied it for moonshine cocktails." Cheers erupted amid the peril, libations flowing freely.

Adam prepared to dash for the jack controls when a hand-lettered placard caught his eye: "EMERGENCY JACKS." He depressed the prominent red button, and the jacks erupted downward with a report akin to scattered shotgun blasts. The RV anchored firm, the winch hauled the convertible to solid ground, skimming across lava and sand as the barbecue enclave succumbed to the earth's devouring maw.

He detached the chain from the convertible, the links clinking in release as he stowed it away. The spare tire swung back into its cradle, locking with a satisfying snap. The hillbillies, largely unconscious now amid the RV's rear, formed a disordered tableau of discarded cans and bottles. Frankie remained upright, mopping perspiration from his forehead, his cap tilted precariously. "Thanks, man. You saved our bacon—literally."

Adam consulted his watch with a glance. "No problem, but I'm running behind schedule. Gotta get to Alaska. Take care of your folks." He proceeded to the driver's side, initiating jack retraction; the hydraulics hissed as the RV rose fractionally before resettling on its tires. The subsurface retained the lava's warmth, yet the vehicle stood secure.

Frankie's eyes widened in surprise. "Alaska? That's a hell of a trip. You sure you can't stick around? We could use a hand cleaning up this mess."

Adam shook his head, already advancing toward the cab. "Can't. Time's ticking. Good luck."

As he ascended into the RV, Frankie produced his radio, static hissing forth. "Grandma, it's Frankie. We're alive, but we lost the cars."

A keen voice sliced through the interference. "Lost the cars? Boy, what in tarnation happened? You were supposed to be having a BBQ, not a demolition derby!"

Frankie flinched. "It's a long story, Grandma. There was lava, and this guy with an RV pulled us out. But the ground just... swallowed everything."

"Lava? In 'Merica? You been drinking too much of that moonshine!" Grandma's tone blended skepticism with vexation.

"No, Grandma, I swear. It's real. The RV guy, he had this chain and winch thing. Saved us all. But the cars are gone."

A silence ensued, followed by a resigned exhale. "Well, I hope you at least saved the food. Can't have a family reunion without something to eat."

Frankie eyed the blackened remnants of the spits, lava still pulsing afar. "Uh, about that… the food's well-done. Like, extra well-done."

Grandma's volume escalated. "Extra well-done? Boy, you better start walking home. I ain't sending no rescue for a bunch of drunks who can't keep their cars or their food. You hear me?"

"Yes, ma'am," Frankie murmured, casting a look at the prone hillbillies. "But Grandma, we're stranded. Can't you at least—"

"Stranded? You're lucky you're not cooked like that food. Figure it out, Frankie. I'm not wasting gas on your foolishness." The radio fell silent, static marking the end.

Frankie exhaled deeply, pivoting toward the RV as Adam ignited the engine. "Hey, wait! Grandma's gonna kill me. You sure you can't give us a ride back to her place? It's only a few miles down the highway."

Adam hesitated, the RV idling. "No way am I gonna let some smelly drunks in. The RV will lose the new car smell." He pondered briefly, the lava's heat lingering in the air. "Sorry. Can't do it."

Frankie's expression sagged, but he nodded. "Alright, man. Thanks anyway." He waved as Adam accelerated away, the RV's tires stirring dust into the breeze.

A few hours later and some miles farther along the highway, Officer Jenkins occupied his patrol car, stationed beneath a billboard's shade. The sun dipped low, elongating shadows across the pavement. Jenkins, a middle-aged fellow with a mustache and a fatigued air, was completing his sandwich when the RV hove into view. He observed Adam at ease in the driver's seat, window lowered, the vehicle hauling a battered convertible; sparks erupted from the car's underside as it grated against the road. The hillbillies aboard reveled, moonshine vessels clinking, their mirth borne on the wind.

Jenkins transmitted, "Dispatch, this is Jenkins. I've got an RV towing a broken convertible, with a bunch of folks looking like they just came from a war zone. Over."

The dispatcher responded amid crackles, "Let it go, Jenkins. It's just Grandma's kin heading home from a cookout. Over."

"Roger that," Jenkins replied, shaking his head. He resumed his meal, the RV vanishing down the thoroughfare, the convertible's sparks diminishing. The hillbillies' boisterous festivities lingered faintly, an echo of the day's peculiarity. Jenkins chuckled inwardly, musing, "'Merica."

Hours afterward, Adam, solitary once more, glanced into the rearview mirror, the desert dwindling astern. The RV's mechanisms endured reliably, the new car scent preserved. He smiled, the rescue's adrenaline still coursing. "One more challenge down," he muttered, the path to Alaska unfurling before him.

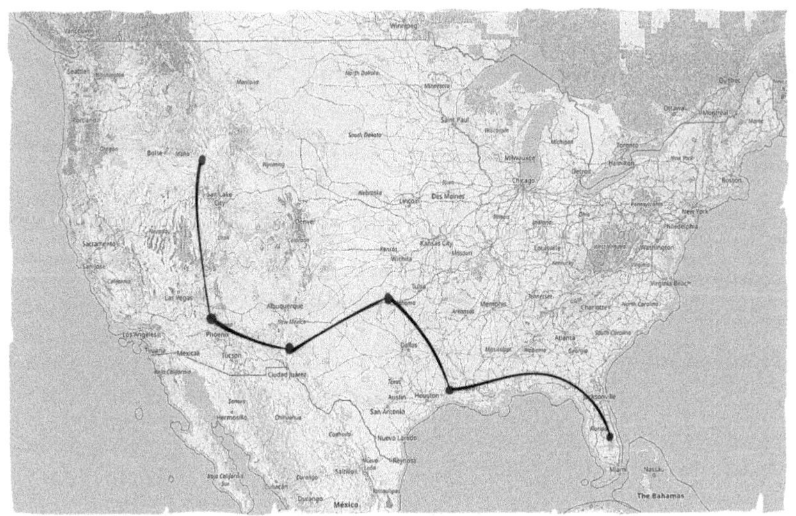

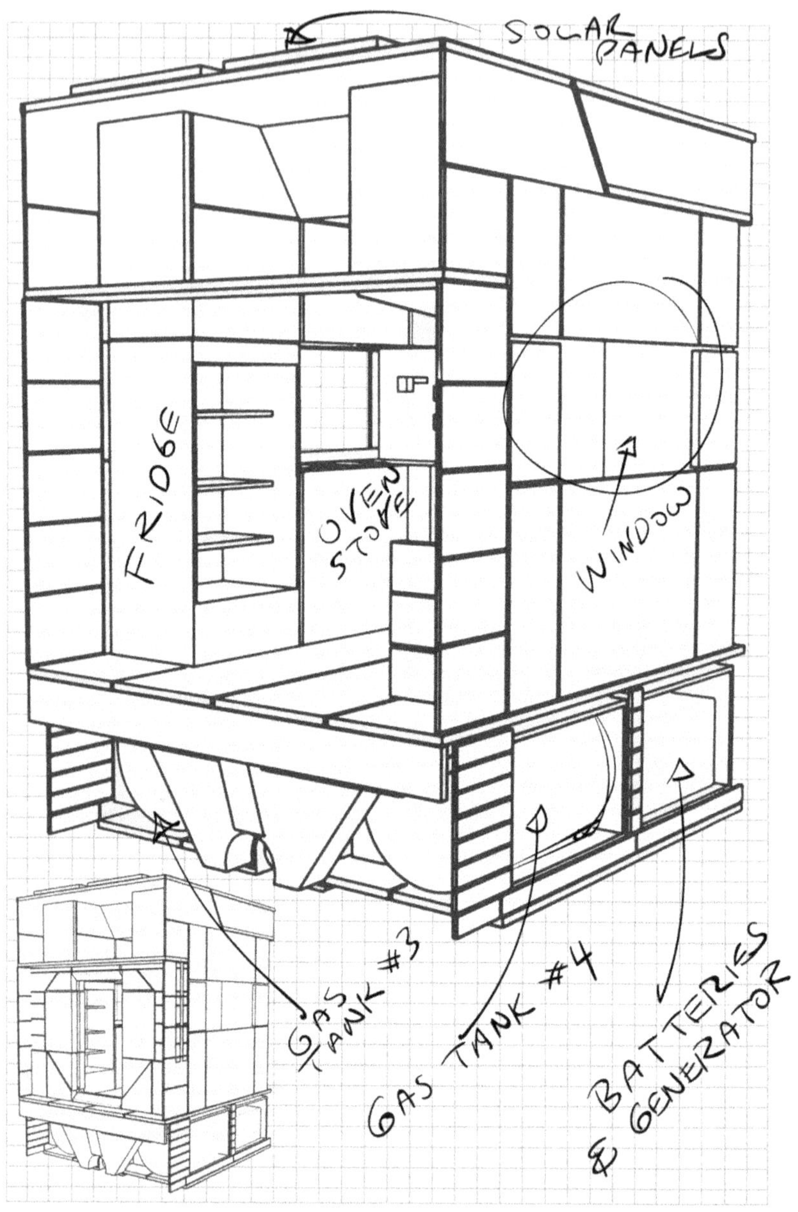

SOLAR PANELS
FRIDGE
OVEN STOVE
WINDOW
GAS TANK #3
GAS TANK #4
BATTERIES & GENERATOR

Chapter 8: Rain and Revelations

The Pacific Coastal Highway unspooled ahead of Adam like a slick black serpent, twisting through the jagged cliffs and thunderous surf of the California coast. The RV, that colossal triumph of human ingenuity, growled forward at an unhurried cadence, its ten massive wheels clawing for purchase on the slick pavement. Late afternoon had surrendered to a brooding slate sky, pregnant with the threat of downpour. Adam's hands clamped the wheel, his gaze piercing the path before him. The extensively altered Renegade danced through the bends with an agility that belied its bulk, yet the sheer mass of the beast demanded vigilance, particularly as the initial raindrops spattered against the glass.

The deluge descended without warning, a torrential cascade that transformed the highway into a gleaming, treacherous mirror. Wipers whipped furiously across the windshield, yet visibility shrank to a scant arm's length. Adam eased the RV to a creeping pace, the engine's low thrum a reassuring counterpoint to the relentless tattoo of rain upon the roof. He had ventured into Oregon by this point, the terrain morphing from sun-scorched sands to impenetrable woodlands, the air sharpening with chill, the heavens deepening to ink. This marked the fringe of Canada's sudden season, and each droplet hammered home the reality.

His phone vibrated atop the dashboard, and he flicked a glance at the display. The static haze had lifted. Ben was calling. He jabbed the speaker, his tone even amid the fury outside. "Hey, Ben. You wouldn't credit this storm."

Ben's voice filtered through, laced with faint crackle. "Adam, you in Oregon territory? How's that RV faring?"

"Yeah, just slipped over the line. She's built like a fortress, buddy. Taking the wet like it's nothing. But progress is glacial. Can't make out a thing in this mess."

"Good, good," Ben replied, relief threading his words. "Listen, I'll be off the grid for a spell. Got to dash between bases for standard medical evals. Won't ping you again till the circuit's done."

Adam's brow furrowed, his focus sharpening on a vicious curve. "Off the grid? Then what's with Alaska?"

Ben laughed, the warmth cutting through the miles. "Chief medical officer here means perpetual motion, patching folks up. Once that RV's mine, travel and quarters get a whole lot simpler. Beats bunking in barracks or snow huts."

Adam inclined his head, the rain now an unending symphony. "Sounds like one epic odyssey. Just loop me in when you surface."

"Count on it, Adam. Keep her steady, no fresh dings." The call ended, and Adam's thoughts drifted to the immense vistas looming ahead. The RV transcended mere opulent mobility; it was a portal to uncharted realms. He shook off the reverie, eyes locked on the slick ribbon of road. Priorities first.

Hours slipped by, the rain unyielding. Adam guided the RV into a fuel stop mere miles shy of the Canadian frontier, neon beacons flickering dimly through the sheets of water. He coaxed the behemoth into the lot, tires sluicing through flooded depressions. The pumps offered scant shelter, but the storm infiltrated nonetheless, soaking him in its unmerciful grip. He topped the tanks, the gauge ascending languidly, the tally mounting. The impending leg demanded full reserves, every ounce vital.

Tanks brimming, he stationed the RV in the expanse of the lot, the vehicle looming over lesser automobiles like a titan among insects. Rain hammered the roof in rhythmic fury, echoing through the cabin. Adam snatched his jacket, hood drawn tight, and plunged into the tempest. Diagonally opposite, a diner lured with its golden glow, the sign proclaiming "Last Chance Saloon" in weathered script, evoking the raw frontier—timbered front, batwing doors, a sputtering neon boot in cowboy guise.

Within the Saloon, the ambiance stood in defiant opposition to the chaos beyond. Walls bore faded sepia chronicles of outlaws and trail herds, tables hewn from gnarled timber. A jukebox in the nook crooned a plaintive country lament, the air thick with aromas of sizzling grease and brewed solace. Adam sloughed off the wet, his jacket shedding rivulets, and claimed a window table. From this vantage, he maintained watch over the RV, though the downpour rendered it a spectral silhouette in the gloom.

A server drew near, a youthful woman with blonde locks bound in a tail, her badge declaring "Number One Waitress." Her smile bore the wear of shifts, yet her gaze sparkled. "What'll it be, sugar?" she inquired, a Midwestern lilt softening the edges.

"Cheeseburger with fries," Adam replied, peering into the blur. "And wrap six more identical for the road."

Her brow arched, curiosity ignited. "Six takeouts? Got a regiment parked out there?"

Adam grinned, the knot in his chest loosening. "Just me and the endless blacktop. Heading far north. Stocking the larder."

She nodded, jotting swiftly. "Gotcha, sugar. On its way. Drink?"

"Coffee, straight black," he said, gaze reverting to the RV. The rain persisted, veiling the pane in cascading streams.

As she pivoted away, Adam's eye caught the bulky emerald rucksack claiming the adjacent table's spare chair. It was battered, bulging at the seams, the sort borne by wanderers of the wild paths. He observed her return with the coffee, vapors curling in the subdued illumination.

"Curious," he ventured, tilting his head toward the pack, "who's the trailblazer?"

She followed his nod, a subtle curve to her mouth. "Some gal thumbing rides, or close enough. She's primping up back there."

Adam reclined, interest piqued. "Who hitches these days?"

She lifted her shoulders, gaze drifting. "Quest for thrill, maybe.

Reinvention. You know the drill, sugar."

He assented, grasping deeper than anticipated. "Yeah, rings true. Seven days back, I was riding waves; now it's RV haulage."

Her eyes widened a fraction. "An RV? That's a sharp pivot. Must be sweet, domicile on the move."

"It's… novel," Adam said, chuckling. "Perks abound. No fretting over a bed."

They conversed at length, words flowing effortless against the storm's murmur. She regaled with tales of habitual patrons. Adam recounted the surge of surf, Ben's world, the bizarre fork his existence had taken post-service. The platter arrived, burger steaming and laden, fries crisped to perfection with salt's kiss. He dined deliberately, relishing the heat, the slice of ordinary amid the extraordinary.

The server eventually withdrew, noting the rucksack's vanishing. The patron had departed, settling her tab sans gratuity.

Adam concluded his repast, the sextet of parcels aligned beside him. The rain endured, the RV a shadowed sentinel across the way. He settled the check with a generous tip, eliciting her weary yet genuine beam. "Safe journey, sugar," she offered, earnest. "Perhaps our trails intersect on the return."

"Perhaps," Adam echoed, pushing through the doors into the gale once more. The portals swung closed, the downpour obscuring all in its veil.

The night stretched nascent, the highway infinite, and Alaska beckoned, a vow etched upon the distant sky.

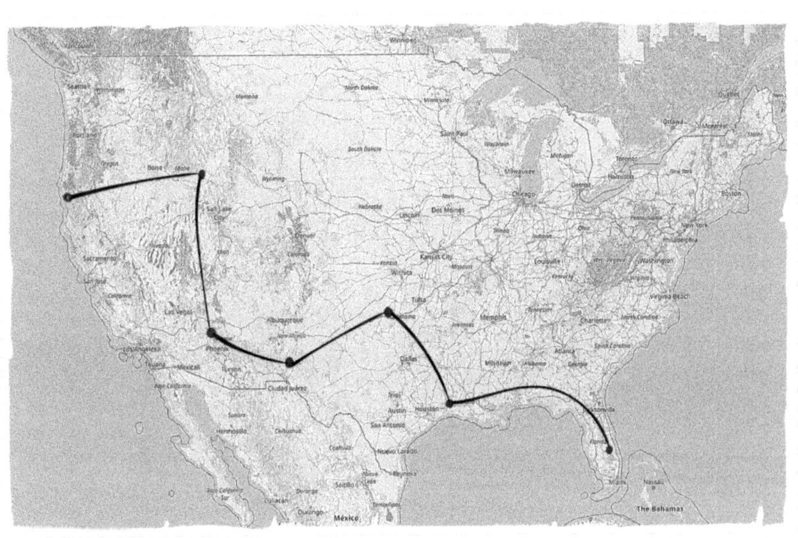

Seattle
Portland
Oregon
Boise
Idaho
Sacramento
San Jose
Los Angeles
Las Vegas
Tijuana
Mexicali
Baja California
Baja California Sur
Salt Lake City
Phoenix
Tucson
Hermosillo
Sonora
Culiacán
Durango
Chihuahua
Coahuila
Ciudad Juárez
Albuquerque
Denver
Colorado
Wyoming
Montana
North Dakota
South Dakota
Minnesota
Nebraska
Lincoln
Des Moines
Kansas City
Wichita
Missouri
Tulsa
Dallas
Austin
San Antonio
Houston
Nuevo Laredo
Monterrey
Saltillo
México
Chicago
Illinois
Indiana
Milwaukee
Michigan
Detroit
Ohio
Louisville
Kentucky
Tennessee
Memphis
Arkansas
Mississippi
Alabama
Georgia
Atlanta
Charlotte
North Carolina
Virginia
West Virginia
Washington
Virginia Beach
Philadelphia
New York
Boston
Toronto
Hamilton
Ottawa
Montreal
Quebec
Winnipeg
Saint Paul
Wisconsin
Miami
Nassau
The Bahamas

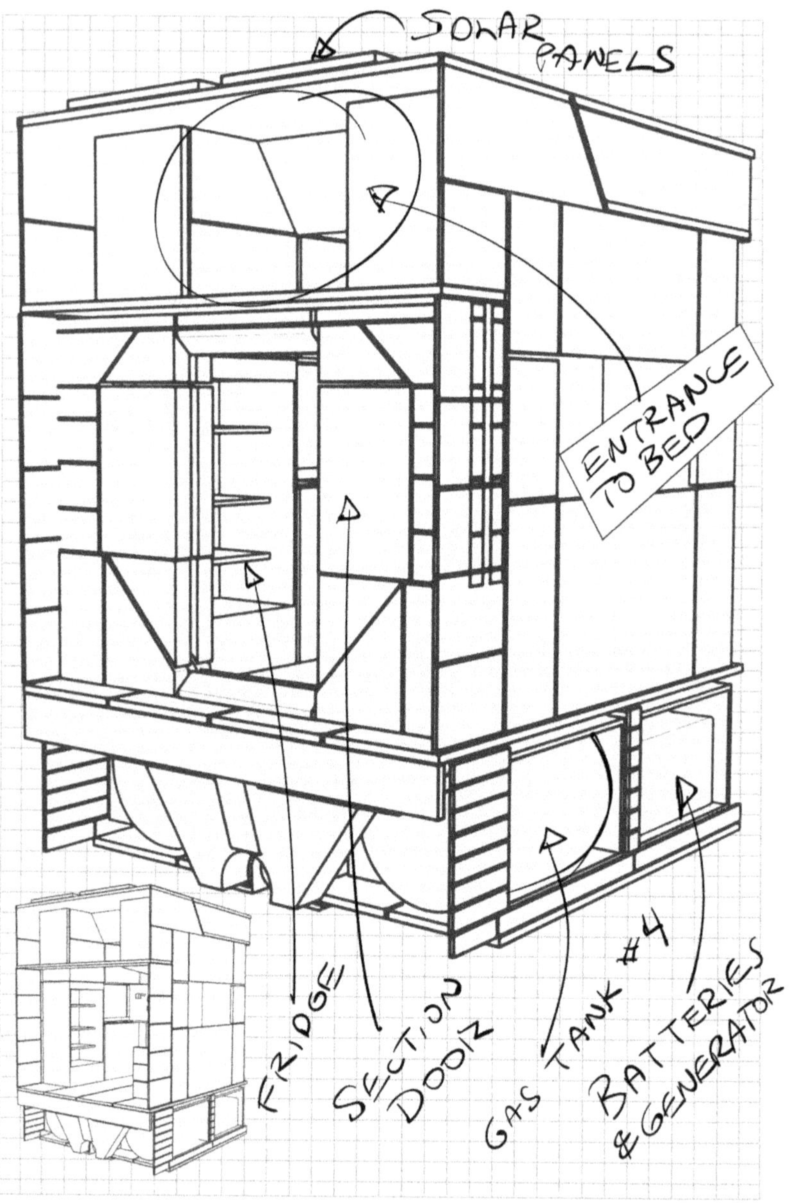

SOLAR PANELS
ENTRANCE TO BED
FRIDGE
SECTION DOOR
GAS TANK #4
BATTERIES & GENERATOR

Chapter 9: Road to Snow

Adam roused to the low, reassuring thrum of the RV's generator, a constant undercurrent to the rhythmic tattoo of rain drumming on the windows. The bedroom lay in shadow, curtains pulled snug against the faint dawn glow. He extended his limbs across the expansive king-size bed, its unexpected plushness a small luxury, and cast a glance at his phone. Barely past six, the wall panel's digital numerals pulsed softly. The interior air hung warm and inviting, a sharp counterpoint to the tempest raging beyond. He pivoted his legs over the bedside, the stainless steel tiled floor sending a chill up through his soles, and made for the bathroom.

That compact sanctuary proved a triumph of compact engineering, boasting a glass-walled shower and a vanity illuminated by the gentle radiance of traditional white incandescent bulbs. Adam dashed water across his face, the mirror clouding faintly in the heat. He tended to his teeth, the familiar ritual anchoring him amid the uncertainty, and surveyed his image. His blonde locks stood in disarray, his gaze weary yet resolute. Another segment of the odyssey awaited, with the elements vowing trials ahead. Yet first, he availed himself fully of the bathroom's amenities.

Clad now in hoodie and jeans, he emerged into the kitchen zone, countertops shimmering beneath the recessed fixtures. He set a pot of coffee to brew, its rich scent permeating the confines, and loaded a compact cooler with bottled water and provisions. The proprietor's manual rested splayed on the dining table, its schematics detailing the RV's intricate electrical and plumbing arrays. He leafed through it momentarily, refreshing his grasp on the control array—gas, electric, battery, generator—all arrayed for instant command. This RV stood as an impregnable bastion, and he its steadfast commander.

The downpour persisted unabated as he ascended to the driver's perch, wipers sweeping in furious arcs across the windshield. The Pacific Coastal Highway had yielded to interior byways, the terrain morphing from sheer seaside bluffs to impenetrable woodlands. He eased onto the thoroughfare, the RV's ten sturdy wheels biting into the slick pavement. Progress crawled, sightlines curtailed, yet the customized Renegade mastered the deluge effortlessly. Adam engaged the radio, a regional broadcast flickering through interference to report inundations and vehicular snarls. He absorbed the fragmented voices, their crackling companionship easing the highway's isolation.

As hours slipped by, the torrent eased, the heavens a muted slate. Temperatures plunged, and come late afternoon, initial snowflakes danced in the headlamps' beams. Adam fine-tuned the thermostat, the RV's environmental systems adapting without hesitation. The broadcast transitioned to a Canadian frequency, issuing alerts for a seasonal inaugural blizzard. He pressed onward, the snowfall intensifying, the exterior realm blanching to pristine ivory.

By dusk, the blizzard raged, the pathway a perilous strand of glaze and mush. Adam guided the RV to the shoulder, tires grinding through accumulating drifts. He deployed the stabilizers, their hydraulic protests resounding as they anchored into the earth. The vehicle rose fractionally, then subsided with a solid, affirming impact. He verified the surveillance array, monitors revealing an unbroken expanse of white encircling them. The RV held firm, a haven of controlled comfort defying the gale.

Adam warmed a prepackaged repast in the microwave, the cheeseburger and fries evoking homebound solace. He dined at the table, the television on silent, the snowfall a mute panorama beyond the panes. The RV's interior heat stood in bold opposition to the nocturnal freeze, stirring in him a surge of appreciation for its mechanical prowess. Meal concluded, he withdrew to the master suite, the king-size berth summoning him. The snow descended unrelenting, a soothing cadence that drew him into profound slumber.

Amid the night's depths, a rap at the portal yanked him to wakefulness. He bolted upright, pulse thundering, and noted the clock—2:37 a.m. The knocking recurred, urgent. Adam donned his hoodie and advanced to the entry, the security display revealing a shrouded form without, flakes adhering to coat and verdant pack. He disengaged the locks, icy gusts surging inward, and confronted a blonde woman, her complexion ashen, azure eyes expansive.

"Terrible place to get lost," Adam uttered, astonishment evident. "Are you okay? What's your name? I'm Adam."

"Debbie. Can I crash here for the night?" she inquired, tone quavering. "I was hitchhiking, and the guy who picked me up got a little handsy. I ditched him when I saw your RV."

Adam's bewilderment shifted to solicitude. "Come in, come in," he urged, yielding passage. The RV's balminess enveloped her, and she trembled, shaking crystals from her tresses. "Are you okay?" Adam repeated.

"Yeah, I'm fine," she affirmed, composure returning. "Just… thanks. I didn't know where else to go."

Adam inclined his head, comprehending. "Let's get you settled. The dining room couch pulls out into a bed. I'll make it up for you."

He ushered her to the dining nook, leather upholstery yielding beneath subdued illumination. The settee transformed with fluid precision, and he retrieved supplementary coverings from the cabinet facing the lateral ingress. Debbie observed, her green backpack yet draped across her shoulder, its burden mirroring her travails. "You sure this is okay?" she ventured.

"Absolutely," Adam replied, extending a blanket. "Get some rest. Washroom is back there. Close the doors on both ends for privacy. We'll figure everything else in the morning."

She smiled, gratitude illuminating her features. "Thanks, Adam. You're a lifesaver."

He withdrew to the master chamber, the dividing panel securing behind him. The snow persisted in its descent, a tacit observer to the nocturnal interlude. Adam reclined once more, the RV's thermal embrace a shield against the chill. Debbie's arrival proved unforeseen, yet apt, an echo that the thoroughfare brimmed with the unpredictable. As sleep reclaimed him, the RV pulsed about him, an unassailable redoubt amid the tempest.

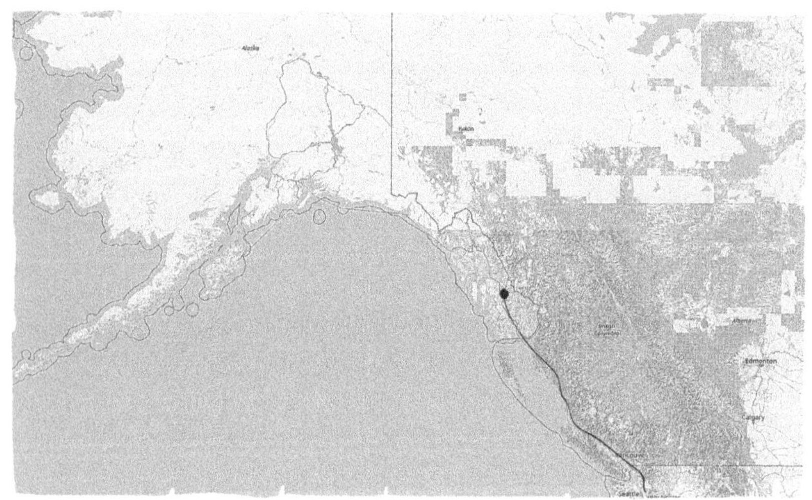

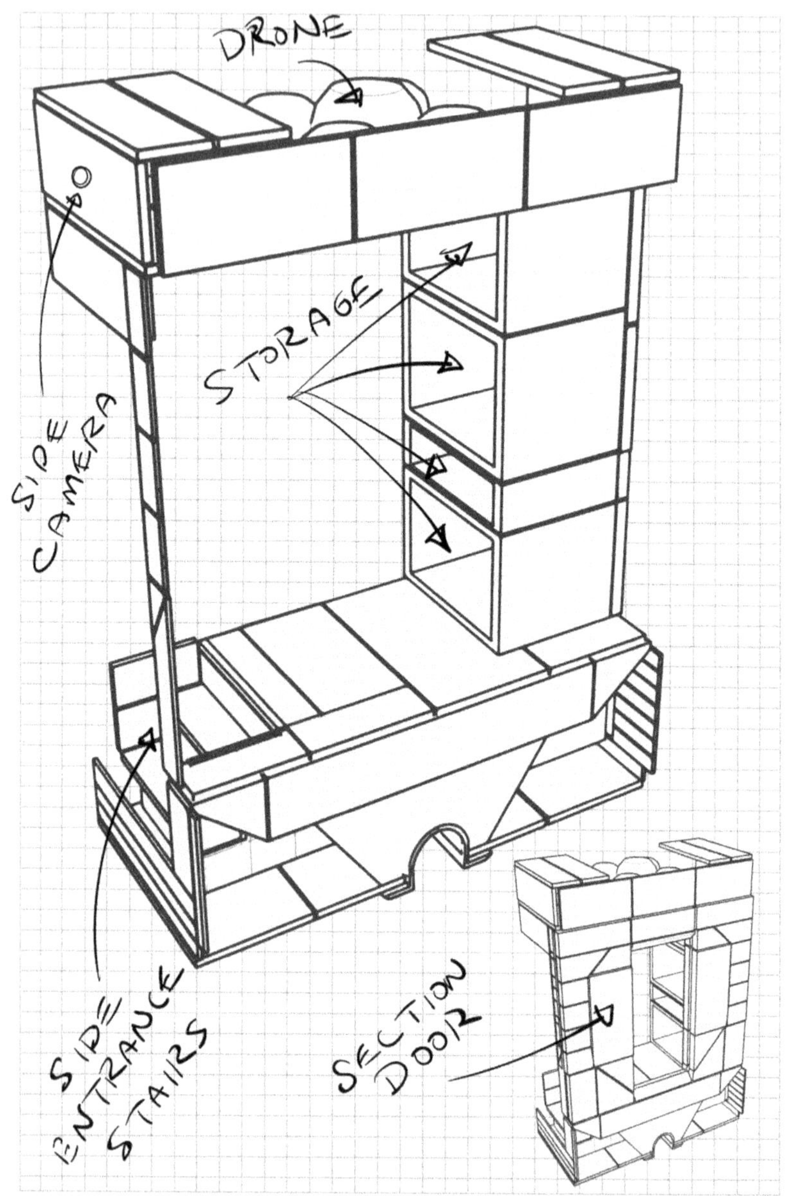

DRONE
STORAGE
SIDE CAMERA
SIDE ENTRANCE STAIRS
SECTION DOOR

Chapter 10: Signal and the Crossroads

Morning light spilled across the Alaskan highway like liquid sapphire, the sky an unbroken vault above the serrated ridges that clawed at the horizon. The RV growled along the slender asphalt vein, hemmed by pines heavy with snow and cliffs of ancient granite that seemed to lean inward, as if listening. Outside, the air knifed through any gap in insulation, sharp enough to etch the lungs; inside, the heater murmured its steady reassurance. Adam caught the rearview's reflection—a tableau of winter's austere grandeur—and felt the old, familiar pulse of the unknown quicken in his chest.

Beside him, Debbie twisted the radio knob with the absent precision of someone coaxing a reluctant lock. Static answered, a hissing surf that drowned every frequency. She exhaled, a small, defeated sound, and the sunlight slid along the pale fall of her hair like liquid gold. "Nothing but snow on the airwaves," she said, the words edged with a restlessness that had been building since dawn. "How am I supposed to hear anything human out here?"

Adam's laugh was soft, almost lost beneath the engine's basso. "We're in a canyon of dead air. These mountains swallow signals the way black holes swallow light."

Debbie flicked the dial again, chasing ghosts. "This is why I live under the sky," she muttered. "Not inside a rolling box."

He risked a glance. Her profile was taut, the fine bones of her jaw set against the confinement she could feel pressing in from every bulkhead. Adam understood then, with the clarity of a lens snapping into focus: the RV was his cocoon, his mobile fortress; to her it was a cage with wheels. He tried a lighter tack. "I spy, with my little eye, something beginning with S."

"Snow," she said flatly.

"Wrong continent."

She didn't smile. "Adam, I'm not a child in a car seat."

He let the silence ride a moment, then offered a riddle instead. "What has keys but can't open locks?"

Debbie's gaze stayed fixed on the window, where the world blurred into white and slate. The riddle drifted unanswered between them like smoke. Adam felt the small ache of having misjudged the moment; he was trying to keep the journey bright, but brightness could feel like mockery when the walls were closing in.

The highway forked without ceremony—two pale tongues of asphalt licking northward, diverging by scant degrees. Adam eased the RV onto the snowy shoulder, tires hissing through powder. The engine idled, a patient beast. Outside, the cold waited, absolute and impartial.

Debbie was out before the brake locked, door banging shut behind her like a judge's gavel. Through the windshield Adam watched her stand in the road's white center, drawing the air in deliberate gulps, shoulders rising, falling, until the mountains themselves seemed to exhale with her. The wind lifted her hair in pale banners; for a moment she looked carved from the landscape, a figure etched in frost and freedom.

Inside, Adam unfolded the map across the steering wheel. The paper crackled like thin ice. The fork was absent from the charted lines—no notation, no warning. Both routes arrowed north, yet the absence of detail gnawed at him, a small, cold tooth of doubt.

A rising whine cut the stillness—fans spinning up, a mechanical cicada. Debbie turned. From the RV's roof a sleek drone detached, panels unfolding with the crisp geometry of a transformer's dream. It climbed on a tether that unspooled behind it like silver thread, ascending until it hung against the sky's blue like a captive star. Abruptly the cab filled with voices—news, music, the bright clutter of civilization.

Debbie bolted back inside, cheeks flushed, eyes wide with delight. "How?"

Adam tapped a switch among the console's constellation of controls. "Drone antenna. It drinks batteries like a thirsty giant, but the solar array's singing today. We've got sky."

She laughed, and the sound was a clear bell in the metal box that had been a prison moments before. "I thought we were marooned on Pluto."

"Not quite." Adam's smile felt easier now. "This rig's got more tricks than a stage magician."

They let the radio wash over them—reports of a winter festival in Whitehorse, a guitar riff that tasted of pine smoke and open campfires. The knot in the air loosened, became something companionable. Yet the fork remained, patient as stone.

Adam killed the music. "Crossroads, Debbie. Map's silent. Both roads claim north. Your call."

Her eyes met his, steady, reflecting the snowlight. Outside, the peaks stood in judgment, ancient and unmoved. The tether hummed faintly overhead, holding their fragile link to the world. The choice rested in her hands like a pebble that might start an avalanche.

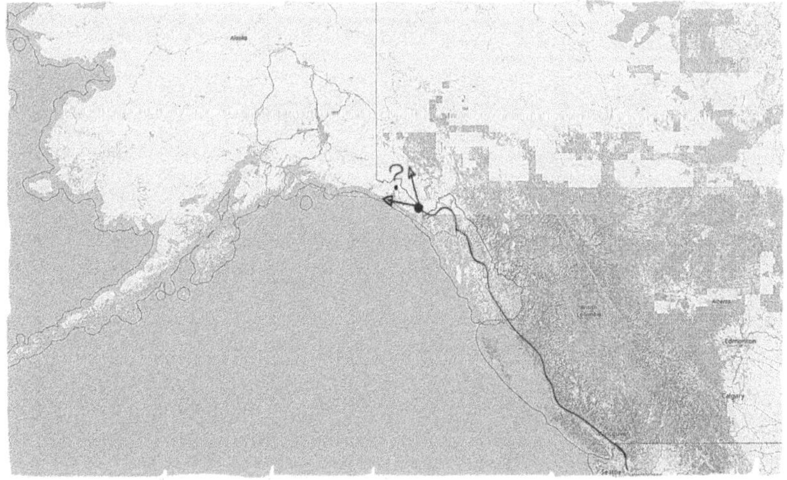

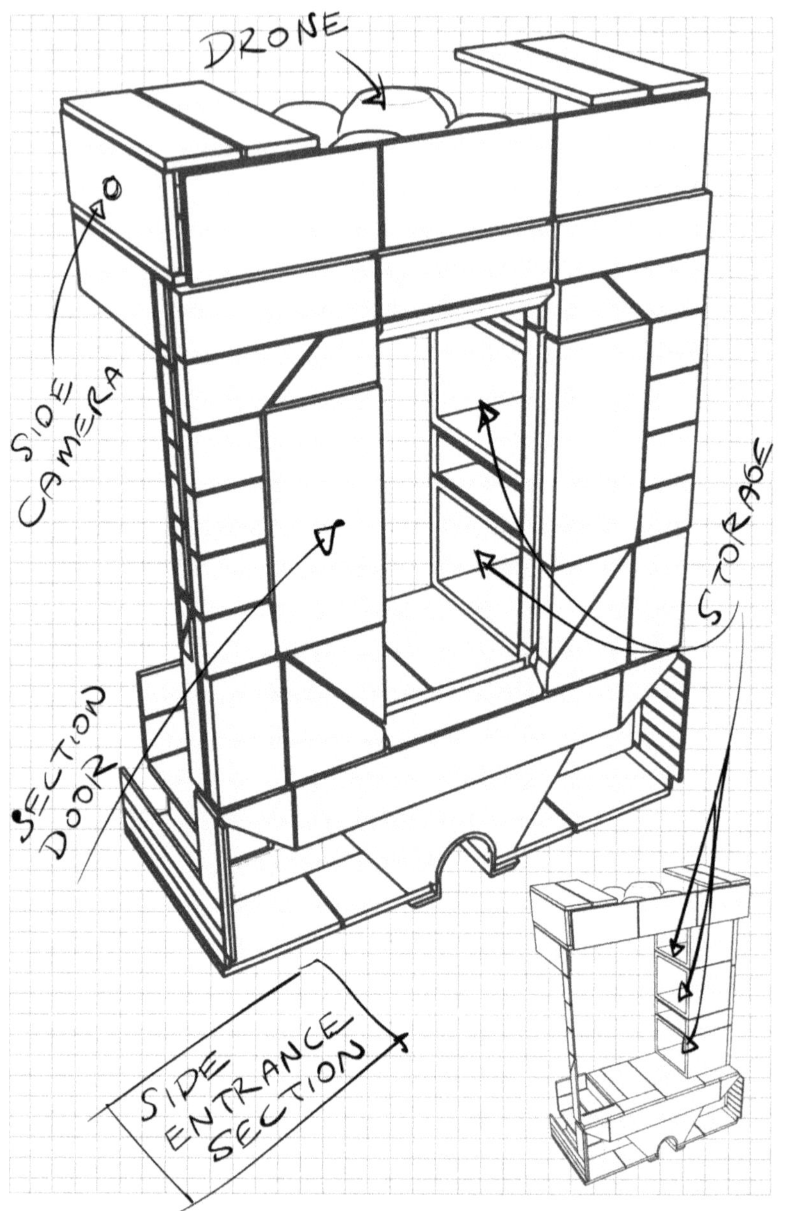

DRONE
SIDE CAMERA
SECTION DOOR
STORAGE
SIDE ENTRANCE SECTION

Chapter 11: Mountain's Edge

The RV climbed the gentle incline, its tires biting into the snow-crusted asphalt with a gritty crunch that echoed the mountain's own slow grind. The road narrowed to a pair of lanes pressed tight against the rock face, the engine thrumming low and steady, a mechanical heartbeat pushing them ever upward. Above, the sky burned a fierce, unyielding blue, sunlight striking the jagged peaks and throwing elongated shadows down into the valley far below—like fingers of some ancient giant reaching for the river that glinted silver amid the white and evergreen tapestry. Adam's hands tightened on the wheel, the Renegade answering with a fluid grace that masked its bulk, as if the vehicle itself reveled in the ascent.

Beside him, Debbie gestured through the window, her words slicing the cab's quiet. "I guess we now know the difference between the two roads. The one on the right continues along the base of the mountain valley, while the road we're on is going up the mountains."

Adam chuckled, his gaze sweeping the panoramic splendor. "At least we have a great view," he replied, the valley unfolding below like a living painting, the crisp air outside sharp enough to sting the lungs—yet within the RV, warmth enveloped them, the heater's hum a faithful guardian.

Rounding a curve, Adam eased on the brakes, the RV's mass settling with a subtle shift. Ahead loomed the tunnel, a black throat carved into the mountain's flank, flanked by a wide car loop and a tourist overlook that begged for lingering eyes. Debbie turned, brows knitting. "Why did you stop?"

He nodded toward the maw. "The tethered drone won't be able to get through that. It's connected to a wire, remember? I need to bring it back down."

Fingers danced across the overhead console, and the winch whirred to life, the tether reeling in with a high-pitched whine that filled the space like a chorus of precise machinery. "It'll take a while," Adam noted, glancing her way. "Want one of those packaged meals?"

She shook her head, a sly grin curling her lips. "No thanks. I'm warming up the lasagna and ribs."

His eyebrow arched in mock disbelief. "How the hell did you pack that up in your backpack?"

"Silly boy," she teased. "Your fridge is fully stocked."

He maneuvered the RV into the loop's center, nose aimed at the tunnel's dark promise. Debbie's protest rose sharp. "You can't park in the middle!"

Adam shrugged, grin broadening. "I think everyone else is taking the other road. I don't think we'll run into any motorists up here."

Peering into the fridge, he swung the door wide—shelves sparse with water, beer, and the Saloon's leftover meals. "There's nothing here," he said, voice laced with incredulity.

"The freezer," Debbie directed, her knowing look pointing the way.

The freezer door revealed a treasure trove: solid-packed with Texas-style BBQ, flash-frozen ribs, brisket, steaks, and hamburgers, a bounty screaming for fire and feast. Adam eyed his packaged fare, then the frozen hoard, finally turning to Debbie as she plundered the spice rack with triumphant glee. "Time for a mountainside cookout," he declared, the words a gauntlet thrown to the wild heights.

Adam stepped out, the mountain air slamming into him like a living force, cold and invigorating. He unlatched the side compartment, unveiling the BBQ grill—a gleaming marvel tailored for RV LP gas, stainless steel gleaming, locking retainer pins secure, three-layered grates poised for mastery, dual-locking lid ensuring safe passage. Adam's mouth watered at its promise, the peak itself a grand amphitheater for a banquet beneath the boundless sky.

11—4

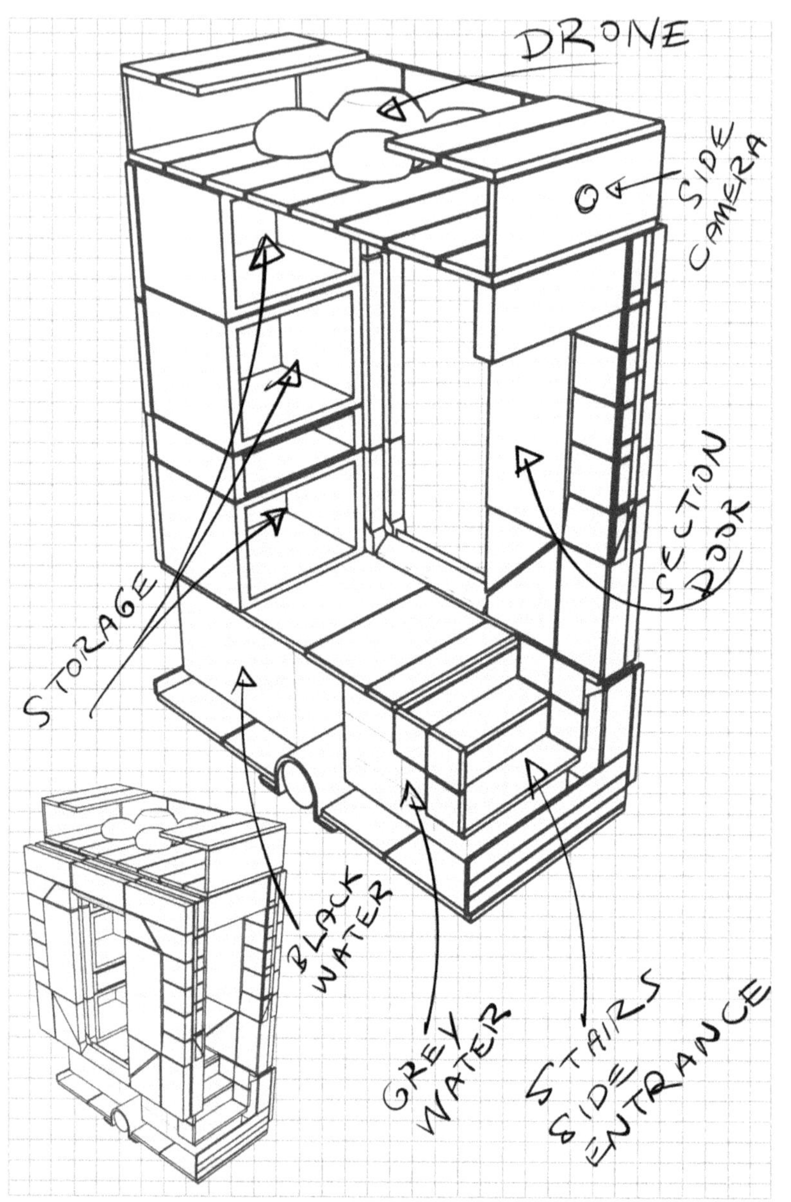

DRONE
SIDE CAMERA
SECTION DOOR
STORAGE
BLACK WATER
GREY WATER
STAIRS SIDE ENTRANCE

Chapter 12: Avalanche's Embrace

They reclined in a pair of weathered lawn chairs positioned just outside the yawning garage bay of the RV, the mountain atmosphere sharp and invigorating against their skin. The panorama unfolded in breathtaking detail, the valley far below a mosaic of pristine snowfields interspersed with stands of dark evergreen, while the river traced a gleaming silver ribbon through the landscape. Adam eased back, the chair emitting a faint creak beneath his frame, and drew in a deep lungful of the chill air. The barbecue grill nearby retained a lingering warmth, its surface dotted with shakers of reaper pepper spice and jars of condiments sourced from a local farmers market, the scattered remnants of their meal a quiet affirmation of the serene interlude. Debbie, her blonde hair secured in a loose tail, released a resounding belch that reverberated against the surrounding rock faces.

Adam chuckled, at last voicing the query that had persisted in his thoughts. "Why are you traveling north to Alaska?"

"Oh, Alaska's not my destination," she replied, her tone light and unhurried. "I'm heading back home to see my family."

"Oh?" Adam prompted, his interest sharpening. "And where's your family?"

Before she could respond, a deafening thunderclap rolled through the peaks, the earth trembling beneath their feet. "Avalanche!" Adam shouted, surging upright.

Debbie tilted her gaze upward, her eyes widening in a mix of awe as she beheld the colossal mass of snow cascading toward them, a vast white surge tumbling down the incline. Adam acted without pause. He hurled the lawn chairs into the garage compartment, the metal frames clanging sharply against the interior walls, and slammed the access panel closed. "Get inside!" he bellowed, propelling Debbie toward the RV's entrance.

She stumbled on the steps in her haste, pitching forward to the floor adjacent to the kitchen counter, where knives, utensils, and soiled plates lay strewn about the sink. The RV quaked violently as the initial wave of the avalanche struck, snow hammering the roof with the force of innumerable blows. Adam latched the side door securely and dashed to the driver's seat, his pulse pounding in his ears. The roar of the snow intensified, an unyielding barrage that seemed intent on entombing them.

He twisted the ignition key, the engine awakening with a throaty growl. The stabilizing jacks retracted with a mechanical hiss, freeing the vehicle. It lurched and swayed as Adam pressed the accelerator to its limit, the tires whirring briefly before biting into the surface. They forged ahead through the accumulating drifts, the RV's substantial mass proving advantageous in shoving onward. The tunnel entrance beckoned ahead, a shadowed sanctuary, and Adam steered toward it, the pursuing snow forming an impenetrable white curtain in their wake.

Several hundred feet within the tunnel, he applied the brakes, the RV sliding a fraction on the damp pavement. Knives and forks dislodged from the kitchen counter, embedding themselves in the carpeted flooring near Debbie's head. She exhaled in relief as a spoon glanced off her scalp, an absurd coda to the tumult.

Adam engaged the rear security cameras, the monitor flickering into view. Darkness obscured all, so he activated night vision. In an instant, the tunnel revealed itself, crammed solid with compacted snow streaked by irregular black smudges of earth. The vehicle's electrical array stuttered momentarily, lights dimming before steadying.

"Damn it!" Adam growled, seizing the handwritten user's manual. "The solar panels must've gotten damaged."

He paged through the annotated sheets, the scrawled instructions a vital guide amid the gloom. Locating the bypass details, he surveyed the array of controls and dials at hand. There, adjacent to the solar panel to generator toggle, lay the true bypass mechanism. "When the batteries run low," he stated, his voice calm and measured, "the generator will switch on to charge them."

"Will that hold up?" Debbie inquired, a faint quiver in her words.

Adam checked the displays for the RV's primary fuel reservoir and the generator's tank, noting the battery charge at sixty percent and gradually declining. "As long as there's gas in the generator's tank, we're good," he assured her, his manner steadying.

"Well, it's a given now," he continued, a wry twist to his mouth. "We take the mountain pass."

The RV's high beams pierced the tunnel's obscurity. As they proceeded deeper, Adam cast a glance at the rear camera display. The dark patches amid the snow were liquefying with unnatural rapidity, the black blotches seeping into the surrounding white. The tunnel extended forward, a route carved by dire circumstance, the mountain standing as a mute observer to their flight.

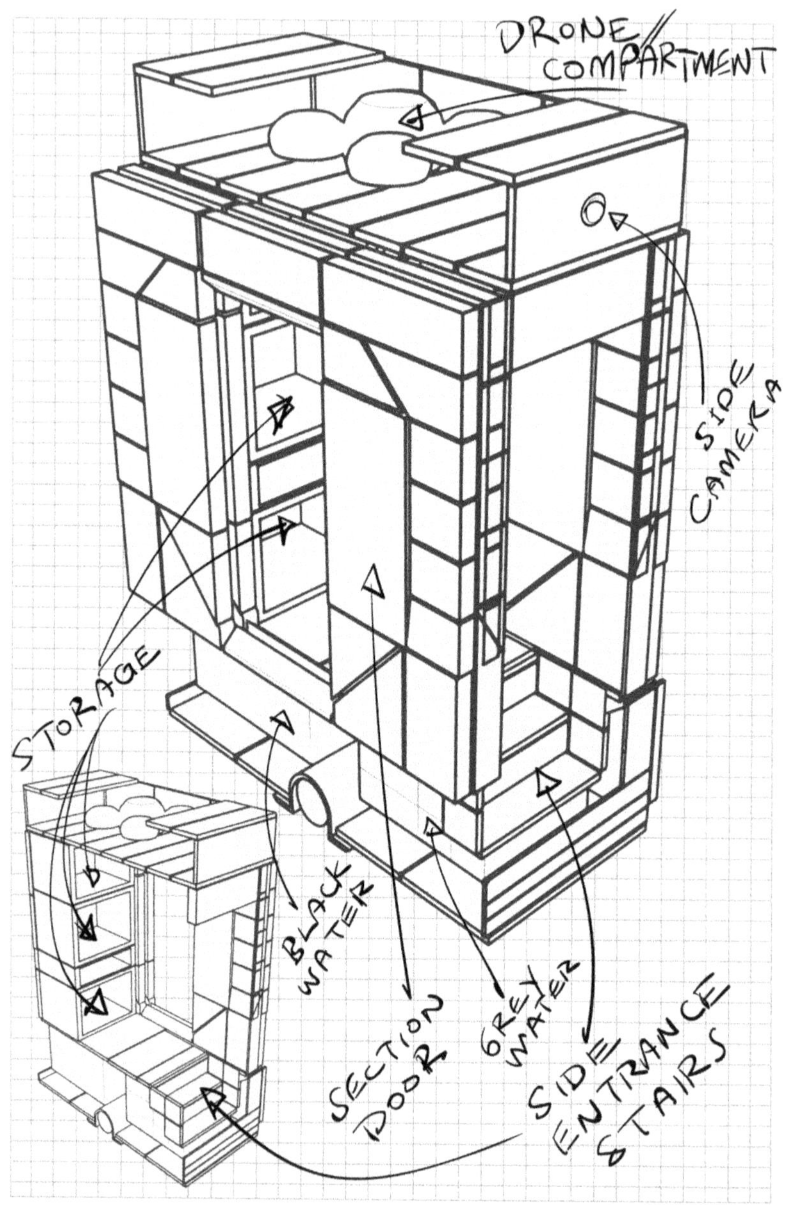

DRONE COMPARTMENT
SIDE CAMERA
STORAGE
BLACK WATER
SECTION DOOR
GREY WATER
SIDE ENTRANCE STAIRS

Chapter 13: Tunnel's Grip

The recreational vehicle crawled onward through the interminable gloom of the tunnel, every exterior lamp and headlight blazing at full intensity, their cones of brilliance slicing relentlessly into the stygian void. Those luminous spears picked out the jagged contours of the rock-hewn walls and the compacted snow that lay far in their wake, a frozen testament to the world they had left behind. Within the cab, the atmosphere thrummed with unspoken strain, the engine's low, insistent drone underscoring the fragility of their predicament. Adam's hands clamped the wheel with unyielding focus, his gaze probing the winding path ahead, where the tunnel twisted like some vast, subterranean serpent, coiling without end into the earth's bowels.

Debbie, ensconced in the seat beside him, shattered the oppressive quiet. "How long have we been descending into this hole?"

Adam glanced at the instrument cluster, the gauges and readouts pulsing with a subdued, ethereal glow amid the cabin's shadows. "Roughly twenty miles thus far," he replied, his tone even and measured. Then, abruptly, "Damn it all!"

Debbie's alarm surged instantly. "What is it? Talk to me!"

"The power cells are nearing exhaustion," Adam indicated, urgency sharpening his words.

Debbie seized the operations manual, its hand-scrawled pages riffling in a frantic whirl beneath her fingers. "That defies logic," she observed, thrusting a section toward him, dense with schematic drawings and annotated sketches. "These cells are rated for thirty-six hours before depletion. We've scarcely logged a pair."

Adam's forehead creased in consternation. "Either the illumination array is guzzling them dry, or there's physical compromise to the units themselves."

Debbie vacated her seat, the manual gripped like a talisman, and navigated the narrow aisle to the battery bay's designated spot. She halted before the couch, her gaze sharpening with resolve. "It's concealed directly beneath," she declared, her voice laced with grim purpose. With deft pulls, she stripped away the seat cushions, exposing a hinged access panel set flush into the flooring.

She released the retaining clips, lifted the panel free, and propped it aside. Leaning in, she located a small toggle and snapped it upward. Harsh illumination spilled into the recess, laying bare the catastrophe in stark relief. One cell had catastrophically failed, its outer shell fractured in a spiderweb of fissures, the injury unmistakable. It occupied the position nearest the entry hatch, where a ragged perforation had been punched clean through the metal—a breach that had admitted drifts of snow and meltwater, forging a lethal circuit that had scorched the unit from within.

"We're in serious trouble," Debbie announced, her cadence steady yet edged with iron finality.

The tunnel's enveloping blackness crowded closer, the RV's exterior beams stuttering in erratic pulses as the remaining cells faltered toward oblivion.

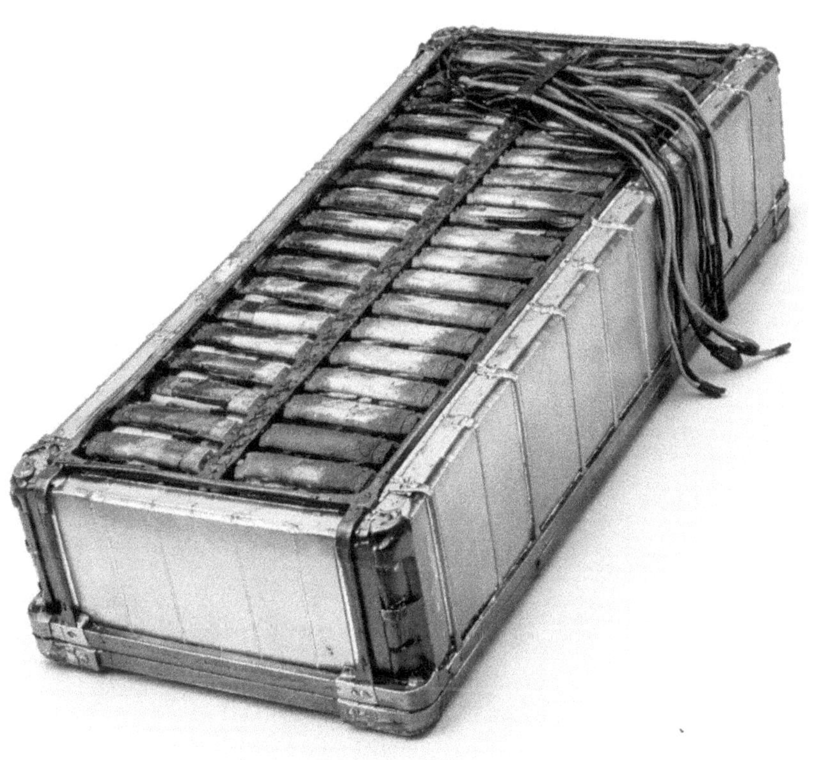

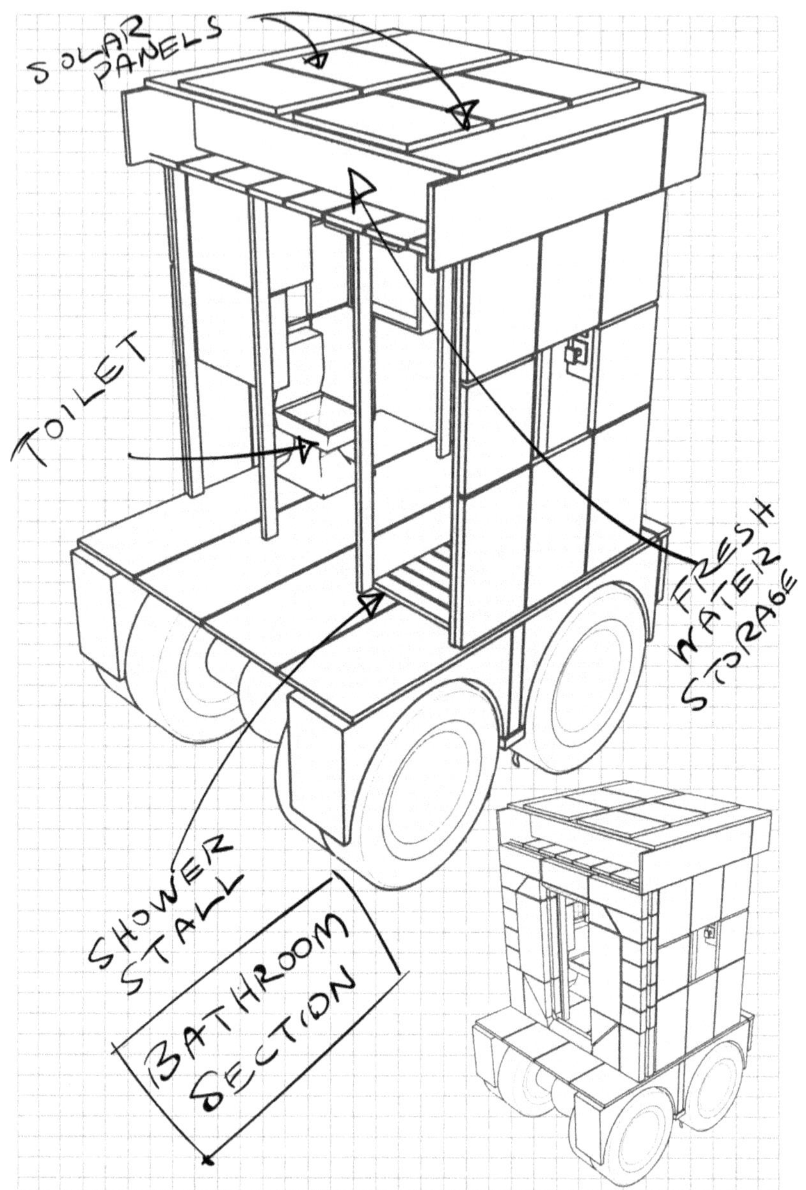

SOLAR PANELS
TOILET
FRESH WATER STORAGE
SHOWER STALL
BATHROOM SECTION

Chapter 14: Beast in the Dark

The RV sat motionless in the absolute blackness of the mountain tunnel, its interior lights the sole feeble beacons spilling faint illumination through the windows into the void beyond. The air hung motionless, the silence a palpable weight broken only by the infrequent plop of melting snow dripping from unseen heights. Adam and Debbie pored over the user manual, its handwritten marginalia a lifeline in the gloom. The oppressiveness of their predicament bore down relentlessly, the tunnel's confines looming like a sepulcher ready to seal them in eternal night.

"The generator should have kicked in automatically," Adam observed, his finger tracing the dashboard indicators. The readouts displayed the batteries' charge ebbing away, each digit a inexorable tick toward total obscurity.

"If we disconnect the damaged battery and close the circuit on the wires, we should be able to stop the bleeding and recharge the remaining battery," Adam said, his voice holding steady against the pressing haste.

"How many hours were on the batteries?" Debbie asked, her gaze fixed on the manual's pages.

Adam turned the manual sideways to decipher the cramped but decipherable scrawl in the side notes. "As far as I can understand it, it was a 40-hour system before it needed a recharge. So, I guess we're down to 20 hours."

"So, we close the circuit, flick the bypass to the generator, crank up the generator, and recharge the remaining battery," Debbie summarized, her tone unyielding.

A moaning sound reverberated from outside, low and guttural, crawling along Adam's spine like icy fingers. "Did you hear that?" he asked, his voice dropping to a hush.

"Yeah, it sounded like an animal," Debbie said, her eyes widening.

The night vision feature of the cameras activated with a flicker, the screen awakening to reveal a shadowy form advancing toward the RV through the enveloping dark. The internal lights wavered, dimming as the batteries faltered. "Quick, grab the flashlights from the bottom drawer in the kitchen!" Adam shouted.

Debbie bolted toward the kitchen drawer just as the internal lights extinguished entirely. "I'm alright," she called back, switching on one of the flashlights, its beam slicing sharply through the obscurity.

"Okay, we'll have to go outside to properly access the battery compartment and make the repairs," Adam said, his voice resolute.

Debbie positioned the flashlight beneath her chin, a mischievous grin flashing across her face. "I'm ready when you are, bwahahaha," she said, her laughter a fleeting bulwark against the strain.

The pair emerged from the RV via the side entrance, the frigid air striking them like a physical blow. They navigated to the battery compartment on the opposite side of the RV, adjacent to the driver's side. The moaning sound returned, louder now, threading chills through their cores. They halted, directing their flashlights down the tunnel in the direction they had been moving.

"What do you think that was?" Debbie asked, her voice quavering faintly.

"Just the wind," Adam brushed off, though his pulse thundered in his ears. He groped for the battery compartment's hatch release, his fingers grazing the chill metal surface.

Adam paused, drawing back from the RV, and aimed his flashlight at the compartment door panel. "What is it?" Debbie asked, concern edging her words.

Adam directed the light onto the panel, exposing four massive claw marks gouged across its face, one terminating in a punctured hole—the very same Debbie had spotted from within the RV. "What do you think made that?" she asked, her voice scarcely above a breath.

The moaning sound arose once more, louder, nearer. Adam lunged to the panel, wrenching it open with a strained grunt. He passed Debbie his flashlight. "Keep the lights on the batteries," he instructed.

As Debbie steadied the flashlights' beams, Adam drew forth the wires connected to the faulty battery and sealed the circuit by tightening the connections with screws. He then toggled the manual bypass switch for battery one to <off> and the bypass for battery two to <on>. Abruptly, the gas generator roared to life, its thunderous clamor echoing through the tunnel, and the internal lights surged back to full brilliance.

"Get back inside now!" Adam bellowed, slamming the compartment door closed. He yanked open the driver's door and boosted Debbie ahead of him. Debbie dashed to the side door, banging it shut as Adam clambered into the driver's seat and ignited the engine. "I am activating the master door locks!" He tells her as the drivers door slammed shut. A clicking sound can be heard all around the RV. Every door, every external panel, every window is now magnetically locked.

Adam switched on the high beams and floored the accelerator.

Suddenly, a giant white abominable snowman hurled itself at the hood of the RV. Adam wrenched the wheel leftward to evade it, the RV colliding with the snowman and hurling it to the ground. All the passenger-side wheels thundered over the snowman, the jolts propelling Debbie tumbling within the RV. She crashed onto the kitchen floor amidships, forks and knives embedding into the mat perilously close to her head once more.

"Are you kidding me!?" she yelled, her voice laced with exasperation and dread.

Debbie rose and staggered to the passenger seat. "What the hell was that?" she asked, her voice unsteady.

"I don't know," Adam shouted, gripping the wheel firmly as he piloted the RV straight down the tunnel's central path.

Debbie spotted a distant pinpoint of light ahead. "Look, I think we're coming to the end of the tunnel!" she yelled, hope infusing her words.

"Finally!" Adam yelled, pressing the accelerator harder, the RV lunging forward toward the light.

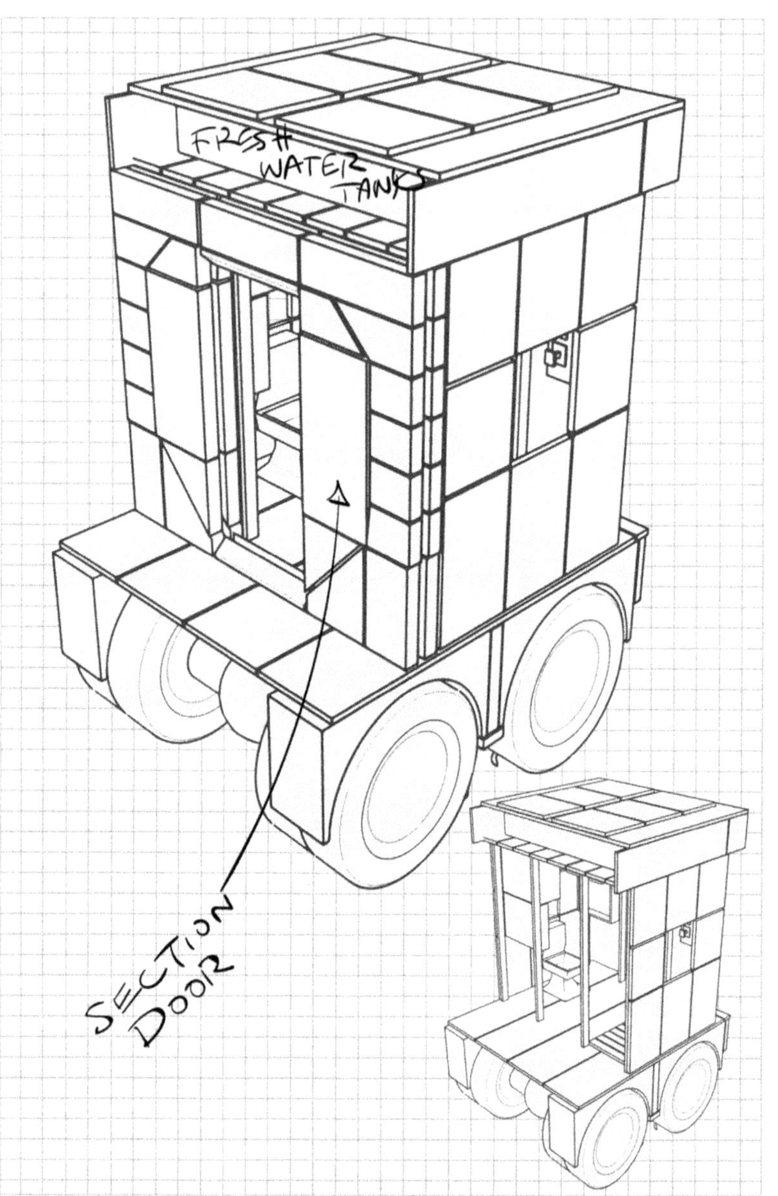

FRESH
WATER
TANK
SECTION
DOOR

Chapter 15: The White Abyss

The RV erupted from the tunnel's maw, surging into a realm swathed in snow. Three feet of it lay unbroken across the horizon, the terrain a vast, undifferentiated sweep of white beneath a leaden sky. Adam guided the vehicle hard against the mountain's flank, the tires grinding through the drifts, carving a furrow in their wake. The road narrowed perilously, its brink a sheer void plunging into oblivion. He clutched the wheel with white-knuckled intensity, the RV's mass a relentless testament to the peril.

"Damn it, I've got to slow us down, or we might slide off the edge of the road," Adam muttered, tension coiling in his words.

Debbie leaned across, gazing out Adam's side of the cab. The yawning drop induced a sickening vertigo, the valley far below a swirling haze. "I think you're right," she replied, her tone even amid the dread.

The RV decelerated, the engine's low thrum underscoring the snow's brittle crush beneath the wheels. They pressed onward along the mountain path, the vista a stark tableau of white and gray. Debbie activated the security camera, summoning the rear feed to the screen. A crimson streak trailed them, stark against the pristine expanse.

"Whatever we ran over, it's dead," Adam observed, his voice edged with finality.

A resounding crunch reverberated from the RV's aft, resounding through the cabin. "Switch to camera 2 for the back," Adam instructed Debbie, urgency sharpening his command.

She complied, and the display shifted to a vertiginous view from the roof's rim, peering down the vehicle's rear. There clung a monstrous, furious snowman, its talons embedded in the spare tire's rubber. Its white pelt was clotted with gore, its eyes ablaze with fury.

"What the hell!?" Debbie cried, shock and terror mingling in her outburst.

"Oh damn," Adam said, jabbing a finger forward. They were barreling directly into another avalanche, the snow on the slope above beginning to stir.

Adam slammed the brakes, the RV slewing a fraction. "What are you doing? We've got to get out of here!" Debbie shouted, her voice pitching higher.

Adam engaged the jacks and buckled into his seat's harness. "Do the same," he directed Debbie, calm yet unyielding.

The RV anchored as the avalanche descended, snow hammering the roof and flanks. When the tumult ceased, the vehicle lay largely entombed, with scarcely a foot of visibility through the front windows.

"I think we got lucky being up against the mountain," Adam said, relief threading his words. "Or else we would've been swept down the mountain."

A chime signaled full battery charge, the generator's whine fading to silence. "Oh damn! The battery!" Adam bellowed. He dashed to the kitchen, rummaging drawers until he seized a cloth and duct tape.

He peered into the battery bay via the couch's underside panel, extended an arm, wedged the cloth into the breach in the outer door, and secured it with tape. An impeccable seal. "Well done, problem down," he remarked, easing onto the floor.

Debbie indicated the rear window, where the bloodied, enraged snowman glared directly at them through the bedroom glass. "A hundred to go," she noted, her voice arid.

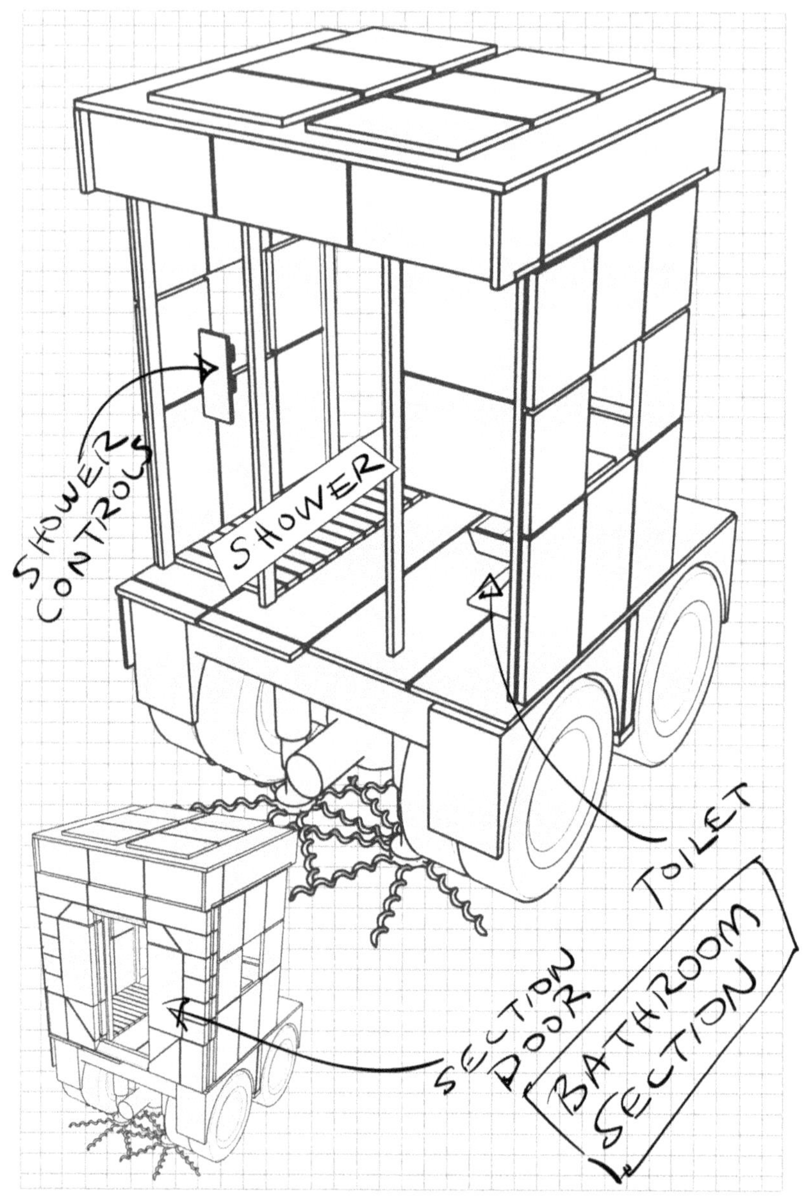

SHOWER CONTROLS
SHOWER
SECTION DOOR
TOILET
BATHROOM SECTION

Chapter 16: Heat of the Hunt

Adam and Debbie crouched together on the worn couch in the compact living room that doubled as the RV's kitchen, the unceasing thuds against the outer hull echoing like some primal war drum from a forgotten age. Every window had been shrouded against the chaos beyond, and the narrow passage leading to the driver's and passenger's seats stood firmly sealed, isolating them in their metal cocoon from the frozen fury outside. On the flat-screen television mounted beside the kitchen counter, directly across from the couch, the security camera feed flickered in stark black-and-white, each blow sending ripples through the grainy images.

Debbie stirred uneasily, her whisper barely cutting through the din. "How long has it been now?"

Adam flicked his gaze to the phone nestled in its charger by the couch's power outlets. "One hour, thirteen minutes." His brow furrowed as he studied the blank signal bars. "And still no bars strong enough to punch a call through."

Debbie let out a weary breath. "I doubt roadside assistance keeps a playbook for predicaments like ours." Her midsection rumbled audibly in protest. "I'm starving. I'm going to plunder the freezer for that pre-cooked pulled steak." She rose fluidly, stepping into the kitchen nook.

Adam straightened, swiveling the TV screen toward himself for a clearer view. The feed revealed the snowman—a colossal, grotesque effigy of compacted snow and jagged ice—pounding relentlessly at the RV's armored skin. "You know," he murmured, "all that hammering has scraped away most of the snow that was burying us."

Debbie located a hefty pan and its lid, setting them atop the stovetop, snapped open the plastic seal on the pulled steak, and slid the contents into the pan. She clamped the lid down, cranked the burner to high, and returned to Adam's side, perching lightly on the couch's armrest.

Abruptly, the pounding ceased.

Debbie and Adam's eyes met in the sudden, oppressive quiet, the absence of sound ringing louder than any assault. Adam turned to the screen and beheld the snowman poised motionless beside the RV's midsection, its featureless gaze fixed with unnatural intensity upon the vehicle.

Adam angled the screen toward Debbie. "Take a look at this."

Debbie's eyes flared wide. "He's just… standing there."

Adam rose, sweeping his gaze across the RV's interior, then back to the monitor, then to the kitchen layout. He triangulated the creature's position with precision. "He's right outside the kitchen. Dead center in front of the stove, to be exact."

Debbie's brow creased in puzzlement. "He's locked on the cooking?"

"No," Adam replied, his tone laced with dawning insight. "He's locked on the heat source."

"Are you certain?" Debbie pressed, a thread of doubt weaving through her words.

Adam grasped the pan's handle, the metal's warmth seeping into his palm like a living thing, and waved it slowly through the air, his eyes glued to the TV feed. Debbie observed as the snowman's head tracked the pan's arc, swinging left to right in eerie synchrony with the radiating warmth.

"Oh my gosh," Debbie breathed, the realization hitting like a chill wind. "You're right!"

Adam returned the pan to the stovetop, where the meat hissed and popped in defiant life. He let out a giddy, tension-shattering giggle, meeting Debbie's stare.

"What?" she demanded, her eyes narrowing with suspicion. "You've got a scheme brewing?"

Adam's laughter bubbled forth, shattering the remnants of their fear. "I think I've cracked the code to escaping this mess."

Debbie leaned in, anticipation sharpening her features. "Well, spill it!"

Adam crossed to the kitchen, snatched a fork, lifted the pan's lid, and stirred the meat with deliberate care, ensuring every strand absorbed the heat evenly. "I'll lay it all out over dinner," he said, a triumphant grin splitting his face.

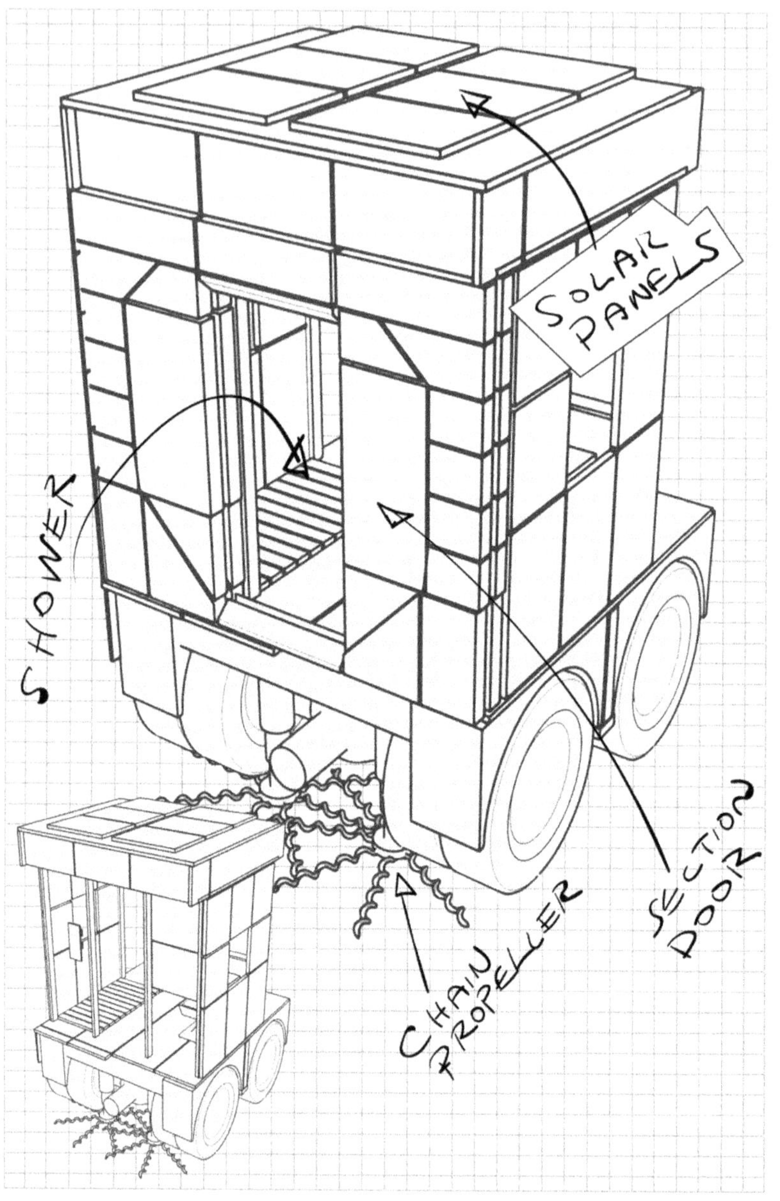

SOLAR PANELS
SHOWER
SECTION DOOR
CHAIN PROPELLER

Chapter 17: Frozen Ground

After dinner, the tension inside the RV hung like a storm cloud ready to burst, the air heavy with the rich aroma of seared steak and the sharp, gnawing edge of terror from the snowman lurking beyond the walls. Debbie's hands shook just a little as she swung the steaming pot of water back and forth, edging her way toward the rear of the vehicle. Every footfall was measured, the metal decking groaning faintly beneath her, until she made it to the bed, her pulse thundering in her ears, and lowered herself onto it, the pot's warmth a fragile shield against the icy knot of fear in her gut.

Adam's gaze was locked on the television screen, where the security camera feed captured the snowman's ponderous, threatening advance toward the RV's tail end. That hulking shape, a nightmarish patchwork of packed snow and jagged ice, swelled larger by the moment. Adam flashed Debbie a thumbs-up, the motion subtle, his breathing coming in tight, shallow pulls. He shifted his focus to the sealed portal leading to the driver and passenger compartment, that solid steel slab standing as their frail bulwark against the frozen nightmare outside.

He moved toward it with the caution of a man threading a minefield, each step slow and calculated. His fingertips grazed the latch, the metal biting cold against his skin. Drawing in a lungful of the chilled interior air, he thumbed the magnetic release beside the lock and flipped the mechanism free, the sharp click slicing through the hush like a warning shot. He eased the steel door into its recess, the scrape a hushed promise of peril. Adam held there, every sense razor-sharp, scanning left and right as the cabin's faint glow threw long, dancing shadows. His eyes fixed on the door-mounted rearview mirrors.

The driver's-side mirror showed nothing but an empty expanse of night. But the passenger-side one betrayed the snowman, planted near the RV's rear corner, its frozen stare boring into the vehicle like a predator sizing up prey. Adam's heart stuttered. He stretched for the jack controls, his hand quivering. There, the front passenger-side jack blinked a red indicator by its release toggle—a harbinger of trouble.

He worked the switches for the others, fingers applying pressure with wary exactness. Abruptly, red lights flared beside every release, a mute wail of malfunction. Adam went rigid, the full crush of their predicament bearing down. The pot in Debbie's grip was bleeding off its heat fast, the metal turning clammy in the RV's frosty atmosphere. Out there, the snowman, its attention waning at the back, caught the pulsing red glow from up front. A low, rumbling snarl rolled from its throat as it charged forward, a whirlwind of snow and ice blurring the night.

Adam snatched up the RV manual, pages crackling like dry leaves in the stillness, slammed the metal door shut between cabin and living space, and snapped the lock home with a final, resounding click. The snowman hit the front, craning in to peer through the windshield, those glacial eyes riveted to the blinking reds. For a heartbeat, it stood mesmerized, the steady flash holding it in a bizarre thrall. Then, as one, the lights winked out, drowning the cabin in black. Rage flared anew; the creature pounded its massive fists against the RV's skin, each blow booming through the frame like distant artillery.

Adam signaled Debbie back to the kitchen zone, the wave sharp yet restrained.

Debbie's eyes were saucers of alarm as she hurried over, the pot clinking lightly when she set it on the burner. She breathed the words, voice a thread, "What happened?"

Adam paged through the manual, hands rock-steady amid the surge of adrenaline. "We're stuck. Front passenger jack's dead. Tried dropping the rest—nothing."

He passed her the book, thoughts spinning. Debbie read it out, voice wavering: "All the jacks are synchronized so that they evenly distribute stability across the whole RV. If one jack is damaged, all the jacks will no longer work until the broken jack is fixed."

"Well, that sucks," Debbie muttered, frustration cutting through like a blade. "Too bad we can't call roadside assistance."

Adam mulled it over, the dire straits sinking in deep. "Could be the gears are iced up. That side took the worst of the drift earlier."

Debbie's gaze sharpened. "So what? Just open the door, step outside, and kick the tires and light the fires?"

Adam weighed it, the risk hovering like frost in the air. "We could lure him to the back of the RV. I slip out fast, give those tires a kick if you will, and haul back in before he can get me."

"Do you think it will work?" Debbie asked, her tone laced with equal parts hope and dread.

Adam met her eyes, the burden of the choice a lead weight. "Do you have a better idea?"

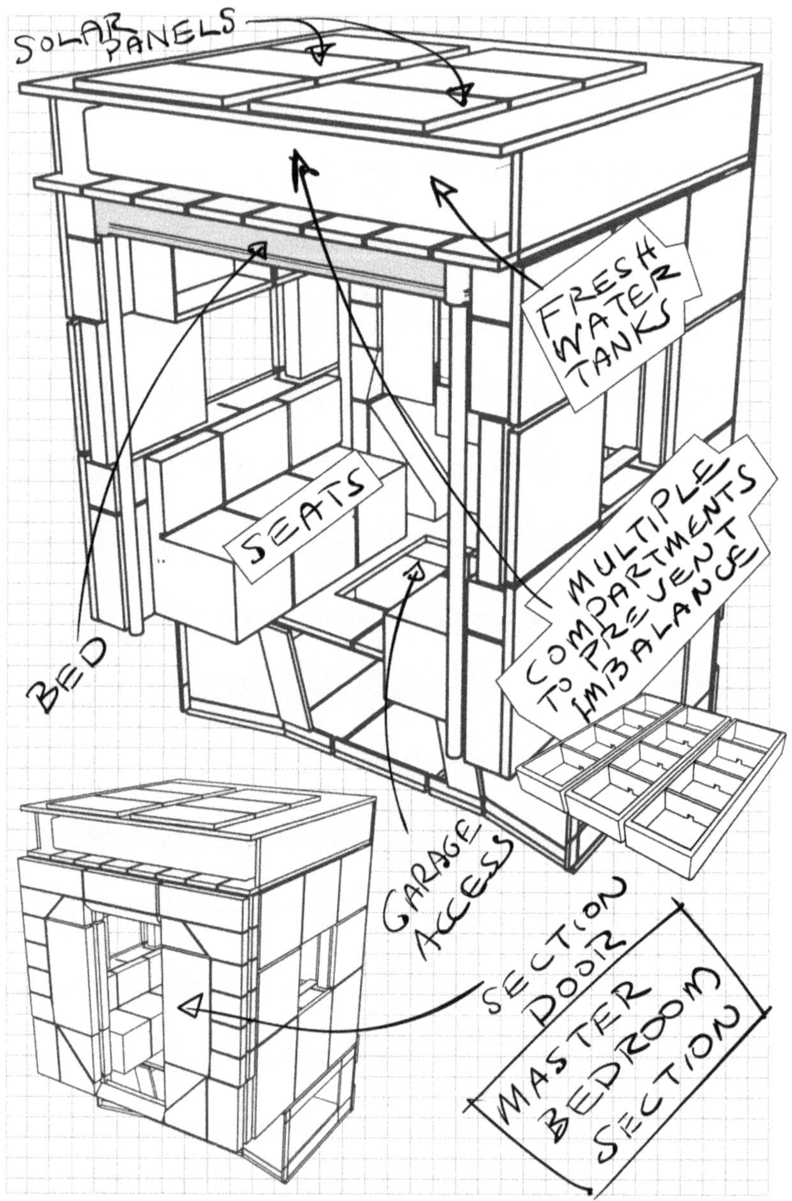

SOLAR PANELS
FRESH WATER TANKS
SEATS
BED
MULTIPLE COMPARTMENTS TO PREVENT IMBALANCE
GARAGE ACCESS
SECTION DOOR
MASTER BEDROOM SECTION

Chapter 18: Boiling Point

Debbie stood before the hot stove, the pot of boiling water serving as a frail bulwark against the icy terror that lurked beyond the thin walls. Steam ascended in lazy curls, a brief caress of warmth in the frost-bound confines of the RV. Adam clutched a sealed thermos filled with scalding water, positioning himself at her side, his gaze locked upon the television screen where the snowman hulked, a colossal silhouette etched against the enveloping darkness.

Debbie extinguished the stove with a decisive twist, the knob's click reverberating through the hush like a distant thunderclap. She adjusted the digital countdown timer mounted above the stove to three minutes, its numerals pulsing in crimson defiance. Snatching the oven gloves from their hooks to the stove's right, she felt the coarse weave bite into her palms. "The timer's set," she murmured, her words quivering on the edge of fear. "It'll take me thirty seconds to reach the bedroom."

Adam inclined his head, his jaw clenched like iron, and advanced toward the sealed door leading to the driver's cabin. The metal chilled his fingertips, a stark harbinger of the peril outside. Debbie hefted the pot, its searing heat bleeding through the gloves, and commenced her deliberate progress toward the RV's rear. Each footfall was calculated, the floorboards groaning in subdued protest, the water's mass both encumbrance and armament.

Adam's eyes remained riveted to the television, where the snowman pivoted its head with languid precision, shadowing Debbie's advance. As she attained the bed and lowered herself onto it, the pot teetering perilously upon her lap, Adam released the latch on the cabin's metal door. The mechanism snapped with a sharpness that pierced the stillness, and he eased the panel open at a torturous pace, the steel rasping along its rails in a drawn-out lament.

Debbie commenced her song, her tones subdued initially, "Happy birthday to you, happy birthday to you…" shifting then to "Row, row, row your boat," the lyrics woven as bait, a siren's call. Adam slithered like a serpent into the driver's seat, his respirations shallow and measured. He registered the bite of the cold, the cabin proving even more frigid than the RV's living quarters, his exhalations manifesting as spectral clouds in the faint illumination. His attention narrowed upon the passenger-side rearview mirror, wherein the snowman loomed at the vehicle's aft, its glacial stare unyielding.

Adam inched his left hand toward the manual release for the driver's door lock, his digits quaking with restraint. He flourished his right arm in a gesture to Debbie. She perceived it, her voice swelling, "Row, row, row your boat, gently down the stream…" The snowman recoiled, startled by the abrupt crescendo.

Adam triggered the manual switch, the driver's door disengaging with a resonant clank that lingered in the air like an eternity's echo. He halted, his vision fixed upon the mirror, the snowman's concentration undisturbed. Adam thrust against the door, yet it resisted, sealed by frost. He signaled anew, Debbie's chant escalating into a frantic harmony. He applied greater force, the ice fracturing with a sharp report, the door yawing wide as a gale of arctic wind invaded the RV, gnawing at his flesh.

Adam emerged with the thermos, the nocturnal chill assaulting him like a living entity. He skirted the RV's prow with stealth, pausing to peer around. The snowman remained at the rear. Adam drew a deliberate breath, twisting the thermos's cap; the thermal disparity provoked a sharp detonation as the pressurized heat escaped. The snowman registered the noise, wheeled about, discerned Adam's vaporous breath amid the gloom, and charged forth, its enormous paws extended, a guttural rumble issuing from its depths.

Adam readied to pour the scalding contents into the front passenger wheel's inner recess, but the snowman closed the distance with alarming swiftness. Adam rounded the bend in shock, and in an instinctive surge, hurled the hot water toward the creature and the earth beneath. The snowman faltered momentarily, its footing betrayed by the instant glaze of ice, propelling it in a skid several meters beyond Adam along the roadway.

Adam tumbled to the frozen ground, struggling to regain his bearings amid the disorientation, his eyes scanning the scene. He spotted the tire, the jack, and the retracted snow traction chain propeller. Clinging to the RV's front grille, he hauled himself upright and dashed back toward the open driver's door as the snowman ceased its glide and barreled straight at him. Adam lunged into the RV, the pursuer gaining with every heartbeat.

Adam grasped for the door handle, but the snowman seized it, leveraging its bulk to wedge the portal at maximum extension. Adam wielded the thermos as a bludgeon against the snowman's claw-riddled grip, yet to no avail. The snowman anchored the door with its left and extended its right toward Adam.

Debbie cried out, "Adam, duck!" Adam folded downward, his body spanning the void between the seats as Debbie met the snowman's gaze and arced the pot in a wide swing, drenching the monstrosity's visage with the boiling torrent. The snowman unleashed a piercing wail as it relinquished the door and collapsed onto the icy pavement.

Adam straightened, seized the handle, and hauled. A blast of wind resisted the closing door, compounding the effort. Debbie shouted, "Shut the damn door!"

"I'm trying!" Adam retorted, the snowman rallying and surging anew. The door crashed shut, the magnetic locks securing with finality just as the snowman's fists hammered upon it. It vaulted onto the hood, battering the windshield, shearing away the wipers in the onslaught.

"Not the wipers!" Adam exclaimed, his tone fracturing with despair.

Debbie, her voice raw and strained, faced him. "You got any more ideas?"

As the beast resumed its assault, Adam activated the internal heating system, programming it for a half-hour cycle, and trailed Debbie deeper into the RV. He secured the cabin door, retrieved the manual, and paged through it swiftly, halting at a schematic overview of the entire vehicle. "Yeah," he declared, a spark of optimism igniting in his words. "I think I have something."

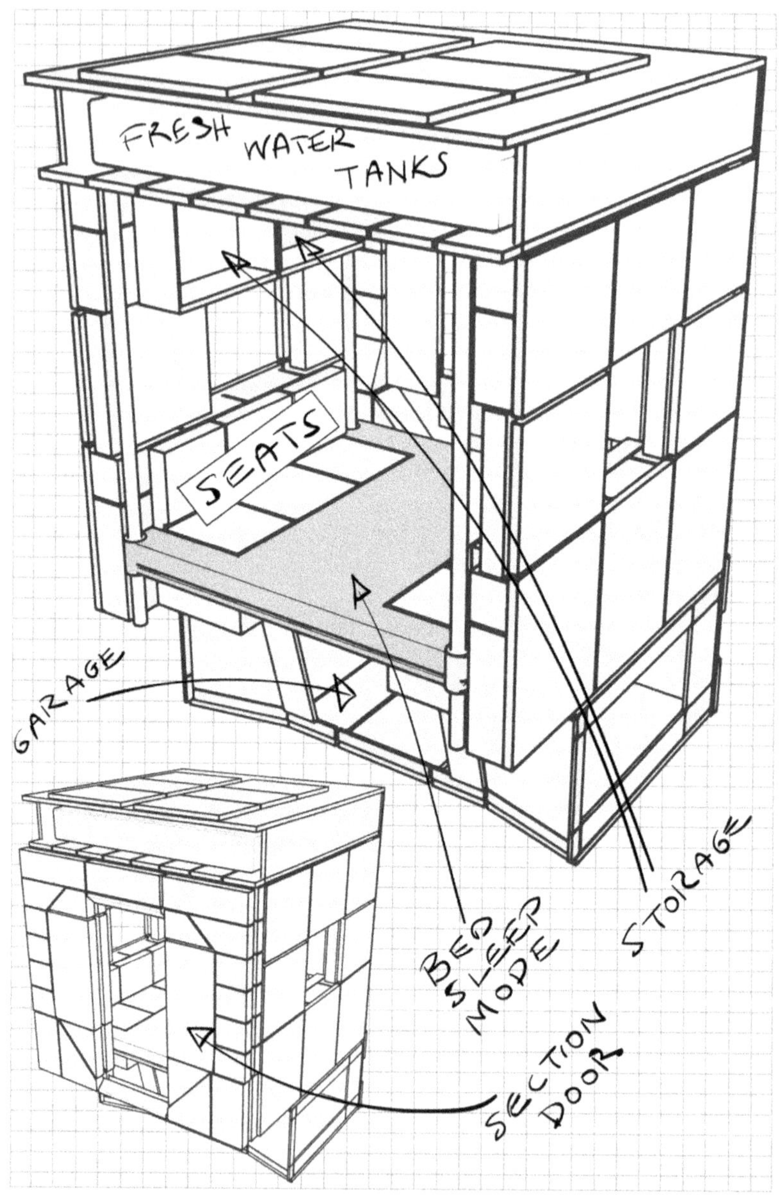

FRESH WATER TANKS
SEATS
GARAGE
BED
SLEEP MODE
STORAGE
SECTION DOOR

Chapter 19: Warmth and Worry

Half an hour had passed since the RV's internal heating system had banished the chill, enveloping the interior in a soothing warmth that stood in stark contrast to the frozen world beyond the walls. Adam and Debbie, clad in robes with their hair still damp from showers, carried the fresh scent of soap and renewal. Debbie reclined against the couch, cradling a mug of steaming tea whose fragrant steam curled lazily through the air. "The place is certainly toasty," she murmured, her voice gentle, a faint smile curving her lips.

Adam swung the TV monitor aside, the image persisting of the snowman striding restlessly along the vehicle's flank. "Looks like he can't pinpoint our heat signatures," he observed, his words laced with a blend of relief and unease. "But you have to hand it to him, he's persistent."

He passed her the manual, his finger indicating the schematic overview as he settled onto the remaining section of the couch, nearer than strict necessity demanded, their knees brushing in subtle proximity. "We have to get going by tomorrow," he said, his tone hushed and pressing. "Our supplies are diminishing by the hour. The damage to the solar panels has reduced their effectiveness down to 33% at best. The fresh water supply is down to 40%. The grey water tank is at 60% full. The black tank is at 20%. The battery power is operating at 50%. The gas supply to the generator is down to 50%. The main gas tank is down to a third. We still have a big distance to cover before we hit the next gas station… and that will be tight."

Debbie completed her examination of the page, her gaze lifting to meet his, a fleeting, inscrutable spark crossing the space between them. "So what's the plan?" she inquired, her voice steady amid the mounting strain.

Adam directed his finger to the tire illustrations in the manual, tracing the depicted lines. "There's a snow traction chain propeller system under the RV, for every tire. Once the propellers are activated, their constant hitting of the bottom part of the tires will most likely cause a shake-up vibration enough to break up the ice on the underside of the RV."

Debbie nodded, a spark of optimism lighting her eyes. "Sounds like an easy solution. We just drive away and lose the snow guy behind."

Adam fell silent, the burden of unvoiced concerns suspended in the air between them. Debbie perceived it, her stare probing his. "What?" she asked, her voice softening to near a whisper.

Adam paused, the admission weighing heavily upon him. "The propellers won't activate while the jacks are down."

"And?" Debbie urged, inclining closer, her tea abandoned on the table.

"We need to bypass the feature that prevents the propellers from spinning while the jacks are down," Adam explained, his eyes fixed upon hers, the closeness of the instant registering keenly with both.

"And?" she insisted, her breath quickening faintly.

"Based on the manual," Adam proceeded, "if I manually change the gear settings under the RV, it will allow the propellers to spin and break up the ice and finally get the jacks to retract. All I need is a vice grip to hammer and loosen the gears to their next setting."

Debbie's brow creased in consternation. "So you have one tire to adjust?"

"No," Adam replied, his voice lowering further, "I have to do it to all the tires, otherwise the propellers won't spin."

Debbie exhaled deeply, the grim truth settling over her. "I don't think snow monster guy out there is going to fall for it a second time. And my voice is not good enough to yell anytime soon."

Adam extended his hand to hers, the contact enduring a fraction longer than mere reassurance required. "We have plenty of meat in the freezer. I think he'll like a steak or two enough to be distracted."

"How will you get under the RV?" Debbie questioned, her fingers retaining the warmth of his grasp.

Adam reached toward a control panel adjacent to the kitchen stove and engaged the switch for the master bed. Together they glanced along the hallway to the rear, observing as the master bed ascended and secured against the ceiling, its mechanism emitting a low, steady hum.

"There's access to the garage," Adam clarified, his tone even yet his gaze locked with hers, the charged intensity of the moment undeniable. "From the garage, I have access to the underside of the RV, without opening the garage doors themselves. I just unscrew the panels that are facing the rear axle."

Debbie swiftly paged through the manual, her fingers quivering subtly, and halted at another section, presenting it to Adam. "The hull of the RV is waterproof," she stated, her voice blending worry with resolve. "Unscrewing the panels isn't enough. You have to get through the seals."

Adam's smile was faint, nearly comforting, though the strain in his eyes undermined his poise. "I didn't say it was going to be easy," he murmured, his hand grazing hers as he reclaimed the manual.

Debbie pondered the peculiar placement of such an awkward access panel oriented toward the rear axle.

Adam leafed through the manual, pausing at a further page. "Aha!" he exclaimed. "It was to get access to the emergency grey water and black water release valves. It looks like after all the modifications, that was the only free space for the valves."

Debbie gestured toward the TV screen, where the snowman continued his vigilant pacing, an ever-present menace. "What about frosty?" she whispered, the moniker laced with both dread and an odd sense of acquaintance.

Adam massaged his eyes, weariness and exigency carving faint lines across his features. He reflected briefly, the oppressiveness of their predicament bearing down. "He's too big to follow me under the RV," he concluded at last, his voice subdued and intimate. "I can slide under to each of the tires, adjust the gears, and slide right back in. But yeah, what could go wrong?" The query lingered unspoken, a wry concession to the peril, yet underscored by their mutual determination.

Debbie regarded him dubiously, her eyes delving into his, mingling apprehension with the instinct to endure. "You make it sound so simple," she murmured, the interval between them electric with words left unsaid.

Adam smiled, a modest, bolstering expression. "It's not simple, but it's all we've got."

Debbie's breath caught, the phrase suspended in the air. "Be careful," she said, her hand lightly touching his as she rose, the brush enduring.

"I will," Adam answered, his voice deep, the imperative of their survival looming like an unrelenting pall, a truth that admitted no further evasion.

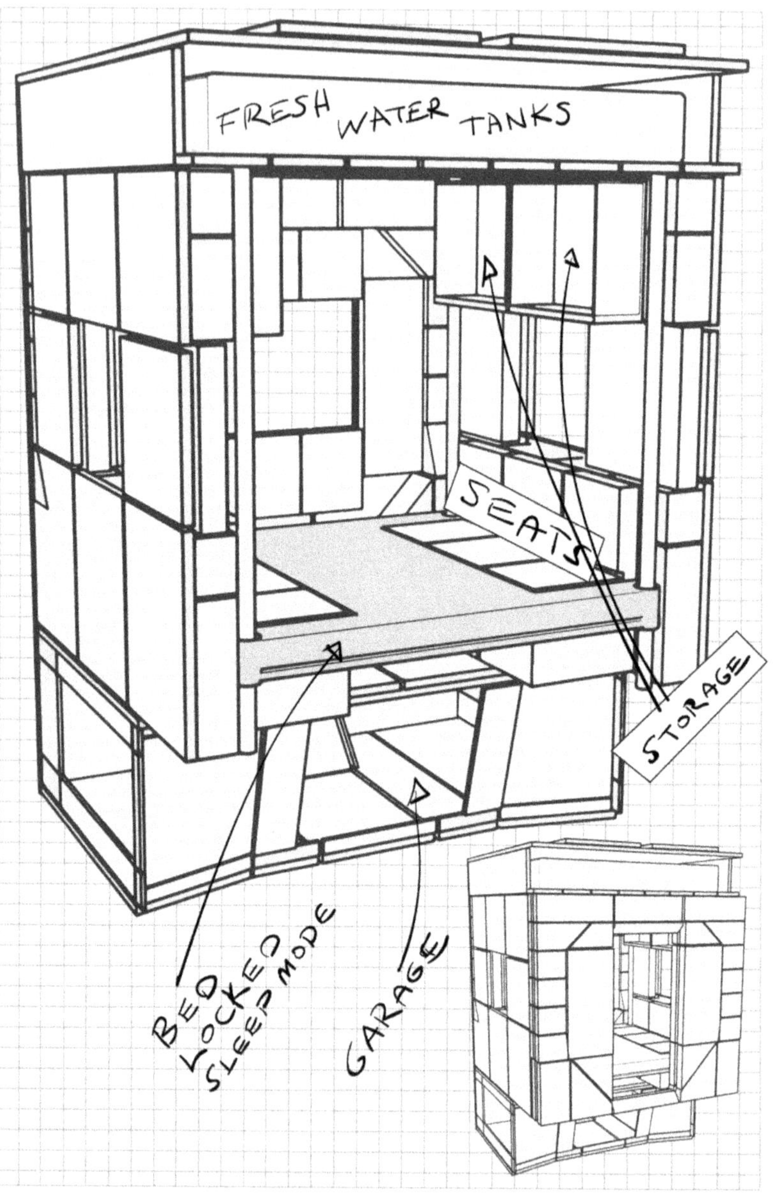
FRESH WATER TANKS
SEATS
STORAGE
BED
LOCKED
SLEEP MODE
GARAGE

Chapter 20: Dawn of Desperation

The morning light seeped through the frost-encrusted windows like a pale accusation, underscoring the merciless chill that gripped the world beyond. Debbie reclined upon the bed perched above the driver's cabin, the pot of thawed, blood-slick steaks standing as a macabre tribute at her side. The atmosphere hung heavy with unspoken dread, the quietude shattered solely by the intermittent groan of the RV's frame. Adam, stationed at the far end where the bed was secured against the ceiling and the panel to the garage lay ajar, embodied a silhouette of unyielding resolve.

Adam extended his reach into the garage, the toolbox a repository of improvised deliverance. He extracted a star-headed screwdriver, its metal chill seeping into his flesh, and eased silently into the garage. He signaled to Debbie with a wave, a wordless gesture amid the charged hush. Debbie cast her gaze to the TV screen, where the snowman prowled toward the RV's rear, its gait predatory and calculated.

Debbie drew back the blackout window screen, the motion a faint murmur in the stillness, followed by the bug screen, its latch emitting a soft click. She released the window's latch and swung it open halfway, the influx of icy air assaulting her like a physical blow. Seizing the initial steak, its blood slippery against her fingers, she propelled it with a sharp wrist snap as far beyond the RV's hood as her strength allowed. The steak struck the ground with a sodden thud, the sound reverberating through the quiet.

Debbie's eyes flicked back to the TV screen. The snowman remained stationary for the moment, its head inclining as though sampling the air, a predator detecting its quarry. Her pulse thundering, she pressed on, flinging the remaining steaks in swift sequence. Thud, thud, thud! The expanse before the RV transformed into a frozen, gore-streaked arena, the steaks rapidly glazing with ice.

She glanced again at the TV screen; the snowman had vanished from the rear. Abruptly, it materialized just to the right of the RV's front grille, frantically inhaling the scents, its attention riveted on the heap of steaks. Debbie stifled her breath, her bloodstained fingers quivering as she gradually eased the window shut, the latch snapping home. The snowman bolted to the crimson pool, ripping voraciously into the nearest steak, its snarls composing a harrowing chorus.

Debbie engaged every window latch, fortifying the RV anew, raised the bug screen, and lowered the blackout screen. She drew a deep, quavering breath, scrubbing the meat's blood from her hands, the residue a stark emblem of their plight.

Meanwhile, Adam labored intently, the internal garage panel his arena of conflict. One screw removed, seven remaining. Debbie swiftly cleansed the pot, the water clouded pink, and scoured her hands, her vigilance fixed on the TV screen where the snowman devoured its feast.

Adam was tackling the second screw when Debbie hurried over, murmuring, "How's it going?"

"Just finished the second screw, six to go," Adam replied in a whisper, his tone taut.

Debbie peered at the TV screen in the kitchen area. "I can't tell how much he's eaten so far."

"Turn on the TV screen in the bedroom," Adam proposed, his concentration unbroken.

Debbie activated the switch, the bedroom TV sputtering to life with the identical live security feed. "Hurry," she pressed, her voice a sharp whisper. "He's almost done."

Adam muttered an oath under his breath, abandoned the manual screwdriver for the electric one, its whine escalating as he accelerated. "Keep updating me on his position," he instructed, his hands moving in a frenzy.

"He's still in the front eating," Debbie relayed, her eyes locked on the screen.

Adam completed unscrewing the panel. He yanked, but it resisted, the seal unyieldingly adherent. "What's the hold-up?" Debbie demanded, her voice edged with alarm.

"The seal's sturdier than I thought," Adam ground out, his muscles tensing. He seized the panel's recessed handles, heaving with full force. Gradually, the rubber seal yielded, a frigid draft infiltrating the RV. Debbie glanced at him, then returned to the TV screen. "He's still eating… it looks like he's licking up the blood."

Adam wrenched the panel free at last, placing it aside with a clang. He snatched the vice grip and maneuvered out into the RV's undercarriage, the cold gnawing at his exposed skin. Lying supine against the ground, he clutched the RV's framework, hauling himself to the first of the four jacks and commencing to loosen the propeller gear.

Abruptly, Debbie shouted, "He's running back!"

"Which side?" Adam bellowed, his heart pounding.

"Passenger side!" Debbie's voice rose to a shriek.

Adam repositioned his body beneath the RV, as distant from the passenger side as feasible. The snowman halted, its enraged, blood-smeared visage peering underneath. Adam persisted, his hands shaking, meeting the snowman's gaze. "Screw you," he breathed, the words a quiet act of defiance.

The snowman lunged to grasp him, its talons falling short. Adam concluded unscrewing the propeller gear, adjusting it to the final position, rendered inert by the jacks. The snowman circled the RV as Adam propelled himself forward, gliding to the passenger side, the snowman now on the driver's side, extending futilely once more.

Adam clamped the vice grip onto the second propeller gear, twisting it free as the snowman charged back around. The snowman attempted again, its grasp inadequate. "Hand me another vice grip!" Adam shouted.

Debbie delved into the toolbox, seizing a smaller one and sliding it to Adam. The snowman, thwarted, seized the RV's side, endeavoring to hoist it. The jacks remained steadfast, the snowfall intensifying.

Debbie peered beneath the RV, spotted Adam at a safe remove, then cried out upon realizing the snowman observed her, their stares interlocking once more; the snowman grinned and extended toward her. The snowman's hand thrust partially, groping blindly through the panel into the garage. She retreated against the garage wall, the snowman's hand clenching and unclenching erratically in the gloom. Debbie sensed the approach of a panic attack. The confined space began to oppress her. She inhaled deeply through her nose, grasped a screwdriver, her hand unsteady, and plunged it downward onto the snowman's hand with utmost force. The snowman howled, a visceral cry of torment, withdrawing, its hand lacerated and lunging anew with its other hand to capture Debbie.

Debbie swiftly extended beyond the snowman's hand and rotated the gray and black water valves.

The snowman twisted its hand and at last seized Debbie, its talons embedding in her arm.

She screamed as the black water pipe thundered and erupted with filthy water and refuse, directly into the snowman's face.

Debbie heard the splatter and the creature's monstrous hacking as the snowman relinquished her arm, and she sprang back into the RV.

"Hurry!" Debbie cried, her voice hoarse.

Adam completed the driver's side front propeller gear, gliding to the passenger front. Just as he secured the small vice grip, the snowman's talons tore into his clothing. Adam wrenched free, sliding toward the rear axles as the snowman dashed around.

Debbie leaned her upper body from the garage and scattered nails and push pins about both wheels. The snowman bellowed in pain as the snowfall grew denser. Adam halted, observed the snowman leaping as if on coals, then turned to see Debbie chuckle, withdrawing into the garage.

Adam adjusted the final gear, released the vice grip. Suddenly, the snowman clutched his leg, dragging him outward. Adam hurled the vice grip, missing. The snowman parted its enormous maw, advancing for a bite.

Suddenly, the snowman recoiled in shock, its stomach rumbling with audible fury. A searing tingle assaulted its mouth. In anguish, it freed Adam as Debbie flung open the side door, shouting and extending for him. The snowfall reduced visibility to twenty feet.

"What the hell happened?" Adam gasped, breathless, as Debbie hauled him inside.

"I emptied all the Reaper spice onto the steaks," Debbie explained, latching the door.

"Brilliant," Adam wheezed, the RV now a haven.

The snowman huddled, shrieking, cramming snow into its mouth. Adam hastened back to the garage, realigned the panel, and began refastening it. He secured a few screws, instructed Debbie to complete the task as he dashed to the front cabin.

Adam ignited the RV, the engine growling to life. He toggled the switches for the snow propellers, their rotation a chorus of optimism. "It's working!" he exclaimed.

"Great, don't get cocky!" Debbie retorted, as she sealed the garage door and hurried to Adam's side.

The propellers hummed, the jacks withdrawing. The RV inched forward. "We're moving!" Debbie shouted, fastening her seatbelt.

Adam gestured ahead. Debbie looked, beholding a larger snowman charging toward them through the dense snowfall, its roars a booming vow of destruction.

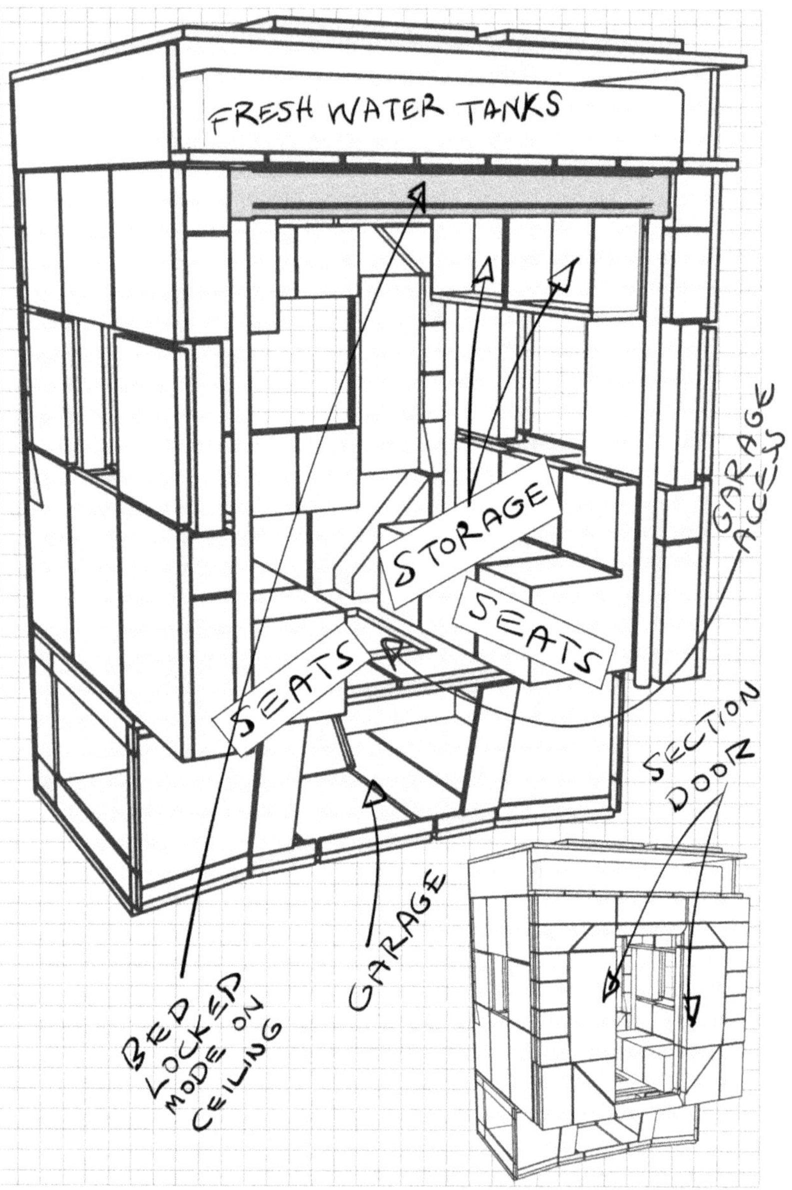

FRESH WATER TANKS
STORAGE
SEATS
SEATS
GARAGE ACCESS
SECTION DOOR
GARAGE
BED LOCKED MODE ON CEILING

Chapter 21: Descent into Darkness

The RV's engine thundered into wakefulness, its vibrations pulsing like a desperate heartbeat through the stifling hush of the falling snow. Adam's fingers clamped around the steering wheel, the leather chill and slippery beneath a sheen of perspiration. He flicked on the high beams, their glare slicing through the whirling flakes like a scalpel through flesh, exposing a realm of blinding white turmoil. Gradually, he eased down on the accelerator, the RV inching ahead at twenty miles per hour, the propeller chains and tires grinding with a gritty rasp against the frozen pavement.

Debbie jolted in her seat, eyes flaring wide, as the larger snowman heaved its colossal bulk against the hood, its frozen mass forming a hideous barrier. The collision rippled through the vehicle, metal protesting with a deep, anguished groan under the crushing load. "Hold on," Adam growled low in his throat, jamming the pedal harder, the RV leaping to thirty miles per hour. The snowman hammered its fists upon the hood, each blow a pounding cadence of raw fear. Adam fought to maintain the wheel's arc, the RV swaying perilously near the precipice, the sheer drop a gaping maw veiled in snow.

"The snow is so thick," Debbie breathed, her voice quavering like a leaf in gale. "How do you know where you're driving?"

"I don't," Adam shot back, jaw locked tight, wrenching the wheel back to straight, the RV bucking wildly. "As long as our right side is close to the mountain side, we are good." The larger snowman clambered fully onto the hood, its immense frame eclipsing the windshield, claws raking the exterior with a shrieking wail that clawed at the nerves. The exterior world winked out, the creature's girth swallowing all illumination, all prospect of escape.

Adam stomped the brakes, the RV slewing in a chaotic skid, the snowman losing purchase, its vast shape pitching from the hood and slamming the roadway. For one breathless, pulse-freezing instant, it skated toward the brink, vanishing into the dense cascade of snow, a mute plunge into oblivion. Adam and Debbie locked eyes, astonishment and fragile reprieve intertwining in their gazes, the instant as delicate as frost on glass.

Adam floored the accelerator once more, the RV lunging ahead, high beams carving through the blizzard to unveil the serpentine trail descending the peak. The path was a perilous strand, its boundaries lost to sight, the snowfall a veiling shroud that devoured vision. Every curve was a roll of dice, every mile a hard-won triumph over the unyielding freeze and the shadowing perils. Debbie's hand sought Adam's, a wordless covenant of endurance, their heartbeats thundering in shared rhythm.

Yet the respite proved ephemeral. The dashboard screen sputtered to life, the rearview security feed capturing a dim shape materializing from the snow—another snowman, vaster, more foreboding, its roars rolling like distant thunder heralding chase. Adam's grasp constricted, the RV's engine laboring as he demanded more, snow compacting with a crunch beneath the wheels. "We're not out of this yet," he declared, his tone laced with resolve and creeping apprehension.

Debbie inclined her head, gaze piercing the snowy veil. "Just keep driving," she murmured, the phrase a fragile invocation. The RV thundered onward, the snowman gaining ground, its outline a swelling menace. Adam's heart hammered, the wheel a contested arena, the road a brutal ordeal. Each tick of time elongated, every bend a trial of spirit, the mountain an inexorable foe.

And then, a spark of promise—a rift in the storm, a fleeting vista of the valley far below. Adam's breath hitched, the RV's velocity holding firm, the snowman's bellows receding in their wake.

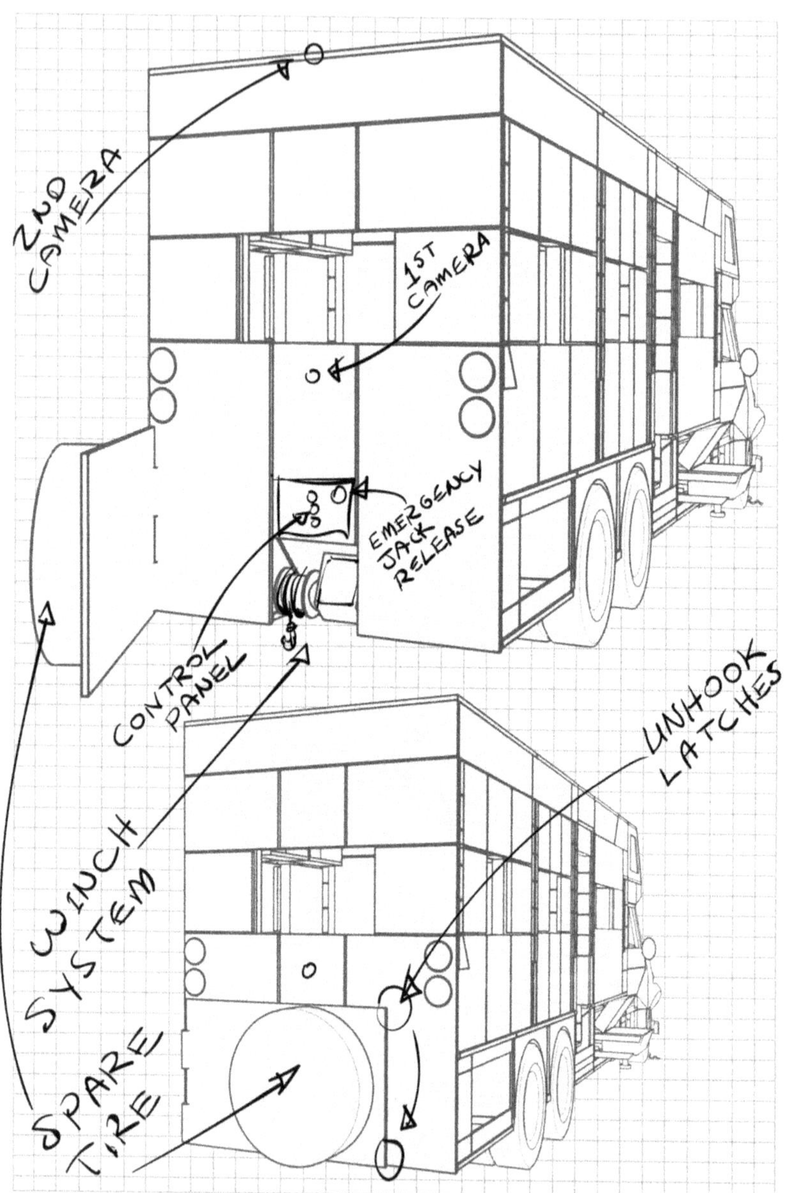

2ND CAMERA
1ST CAMERA
EMERGENCY JACK RELEASE
CONTROL PANEL
WINCH SYSTEM
SPARE TIRE
UNHOOK LATCHES

Chapter 22: Icebound Inferno

The recreational vehicle thundered downward along the winding mountain track, its descent gradually flattening out onto the perilous sweep of a frozen lake, a vast sheet of ice that mirrored the sullen gray overcast above like some immense, unblinking eye. Adam's fingers clenched the steering wheel, the leather grown slippery beneath his palms from the sheen of perspiration, while the drone was sent aloft once more, its subdued whirring a slender thread of assurance amid the isolation. The radio sputtered into activity, fragments of local bulletins and melodies spilling from the speakers, a momentary balm against the encroaching horror. Debbie's countenance brightened, an uncommon smile piercing the veil of strain that had settled over her features.

Adam extended a hand toward the telephone, punching in Ben's number, the ringing tone a fragile conduit through the encompassing quiet. It chimed several times before yielding to the impersonal greeting of voicemail. "Damn it," Adam growled under his breath, his tone taut as wire. "He's still incommunicado."

Abruptly, every link to the outside world vanished. The radio fell silent, the telephone's display winked out into darkness, and a hiss of static slithered forth like the warning of some poisonous serpent. Adam fixed his gaze upon the inert device, his forehead creasing in bafflement. "What the hell just happened?"

Ere39 he could frame a reply, a titanic collision rocked the vehicle, the flank buckling inward as though struck by the bulk of a snowman hurling its frozen mass against them. The RV veered wildly from the roadway, slewing across the ice in a vortex of whiteness and dread. Debbie cried out, "What the hell happened?" her words a piercing wail of alarm.

Adam jabbed at controls in a frenzy, the security monitors flickering to life upon the instrument panel. Together they peered at a secondary display, discerning a hulking, pallid shape bearing down upon them with relentless intent. Adam and Debbie turned their eyes to the passenger-side rearview mirror, confronting a vision from the depths of nightmare: a snowman loping on all fours, each bound splintering the ice beneath it, a hunter closing the gap with predatory fury.

"We've got to get out of here," Debbie murmured, her voice quivering like a leaf in the gale.

"Yeah, I think you're right," Adam replied, his words measured despite the turmoil. He wrenched the wheel, depressing the accelerator; the RV's tires spun uselessly for an instant before the propeller chains bit into the surface, propelling them forward mere moments ahead of the pursuer. The snowman lunged, its enormous frame seizing the spare tire mounted at the rear and locking on with unyielding force, the added mass fracturing the ice in a web of cracks. The vehicle slewed to a halt, its wheels finding no purchase on the disintegrating frozen plain, as the snowman clambered upward, hammering upon the roof with blows that hastened the ice's demise. The RV commenced its slow subsidence, frigid water rising to caress the tires.

Debbie's gaze, fraught with desperation and entreaty, locked upon Adam's—a wordless supplication for deliverance.

Adam favored her with a smile and declared, "Don't worry, the RV is waterproof."

Debbie cleared her throat with a pointed gesture toward the rear compartment, where the bedroom lay exposed to the encroaching flood. "I didn't think I had to screw back all the screws. Who knew?"

Adam swiftly actuated one of the door mechanisms. They observed the bedroom portal sliding shut, yet the water persisted in infiltrating the forward sections through unseen crevices.

"Damn it!" Adam vaulted from his seat, dashing to the galley area and snatching the largest blade available, its edge catching the faint illumination in a brief gleam. He released the roof access panel; a ladder descended, unfolding from the overhead like a precarious salvation. "Come on! Follow me!" he bellowed, ascending with haste, the biting chill of the exterior air gnawing at his exposed flesh.

Debbie hauled herself onto the roof, clutching Adam's left leg for anchorage as the snowman drew nearer, its guttural roars resounding like rolling thunder. Adam slashed at the drone's anchoring line, the cable proving stubbornly resilient while the snowman balanced itself and advanced inexorably. "Hold on to me for dear life!" Adam roared, the line at last parting; he coiled his arm about the severed tether as the drone hoisted them skyward. The snowman's claws grazed mere inches from Debbie's boots, crashing down upon the RV's roof as the ice at last gave way, plunging the vehicle and its assail3 monstrous occupant into the abyssal cold below.

The drone's trajectory curved in a graceful arc, attaining its zenith before commencing a controlled descent toward the distant terrain, well removed from the submerging RV. Adam and Debbie struck the ground with bone-jarring force, the drone itself shattering against proximate boulders. They lurched upright, a medical helicopter materializing from the heavens, its blades whipping the air into a vortex of optimism.

Ben emerged, arms flung wide in exuberant welcome, his smile expansive as that of some fabled feline. "Ben? What are you doing here?" Adam inquired, his voice laced with astonishment and a thread of vexation.

Ben enveloped Adam in an embrace, then clasped Debbie's hand with theatrical fervor. "That was amazing!" he exclaimed, his tone bubbling with unbridled enthusiasm.

"What are you talking about?" Adam pressed, casting a glance at Debbie before returning his attention to Ben.

Ben extracted his telephone, displaying his social media profile, where the live broadcast teemed with an audience numbering in the millions. "You're the biggest social media star ever! The live streaming monetization is huge!"

Adam regarded Debbie, then shifted his stare back to Ben. "Wait, we were content fodder for you?" Debbie demanded, her words infused with a blend of fury and disbelief.

Ben chuckled, the sound incongruously buoyant given the circumstances, as he seized them by the shoulders and propelled them toward the awaiting aircraft. "No! The live feed was activated when the RV was initially driven out of Charlie's. The security camera feeds, outside and inside, were streaming to my social media account. I thought I had set it to private, but it defaulted to public. That's why you were having a hard time with communications and radio. The live feed was eating up the bandwidth and killing the batteries."

"Why didn't you tell me this when we were on the phone?" Adam asked, his inflection edged with sharpness.

Ben assisted Debbie aboard the helicopter, his grin undimmed. "I didn't know until a couple of hours ago, when I got back from my tour and clicked on my alerts. You can imagine my surprise seeing you two fighting for your lives."

Adam clambered into the cabin, a sardonic chuckle escaping his lips. Ben secured the door, his voice elevating to compete with the rotor's clamor. "I grabbed the first helicopter I could get my hands on and tracked you down here. The money from the live feed is huge, did I tell you?"

"Sorry I couldn't deliver it to you," Adam retorted, his tone arid as desert sands. "I ran into a little bit of some problems."

Ben tittered, signaling the pilot to ascend. "That's okay. We have more than enough money to get another custom job. Heck, a whole fleet of them!"

Adam exchanged a look with Debbie, her brows arched in wry acceptance, a subtle nod of capitulation as the helicopter soared aloft, abandoning the wreckage of the drone, the submerged RV, and the snowman entombed in the glacial depths far beneath.

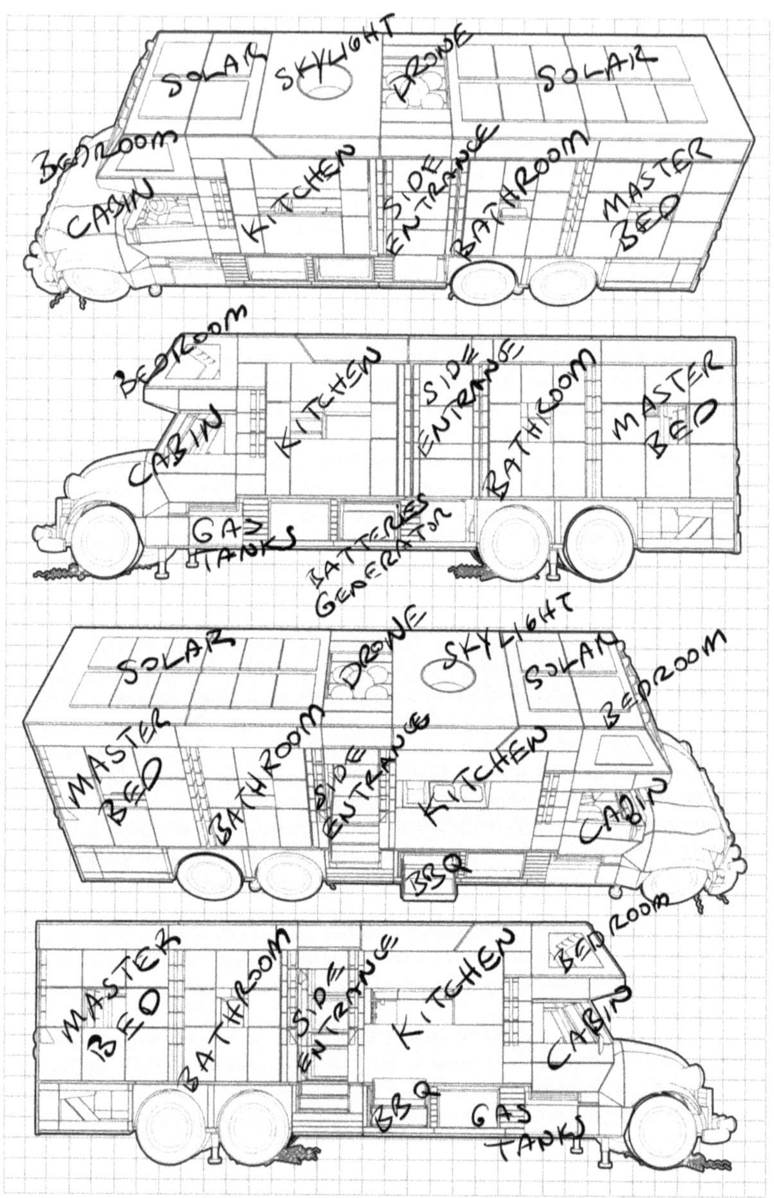
SOLAR
SKYLIGHT
DRONE
SOLAR
BEDROOM
CABIN
KITCHEN
SIDE ENTRANCE
BATHROOM
MASTER BED
BEDROOM
CABIN
KITCHEN
SIDE ENTRANCE
BATHROOM
MASTER BED
GAS TANKS
BATTERIES
GENERATOR
SOLAR
DRONE
SKYLIGHT
SOLAR
MASTER BED
BATHROOM
SIDE ENTRANCE
KITCHEN
BEDROOM
CABIN
BBQ
MASTER BED
BATHROOM
SIDE ENTRANCE
KITCHEN
BEDROOM
CABIN
BBQ
GAS TANKS

Chapter 23: Beyond the Horizon

Months had slipped past like meltwater from a glacier, and now the Florida sun hammered down outside with the unrelenting force of a fusion reactor, a far cry from the bone-numbing chill that still haunted the edges of their Alaskan memories. Adam lounged in the sumptuous confines of the Chase Coach waiting lounge, the air-conditioning humming like a distant hive of contented machines, its cool breath a soothing caress against his skin. He nursed his tea, watching the steam rise in lazy, ethereal spirals that evoked half-forgotten ghosts, while his eyes traced the intricate schematics for RV 2.0 on the tablet before him—pages woven with the intricate threads of engineering possibility and untapped potential. A notification chimed softly, Debbie's message flickering into existence like a starburst in the quiet: "Ben's dropping by. What do you want for dinner? Subs or potato lasagna?" Adam's lips curved in a quiet smile, the decision effortless. "Steaks," he tapped out, the simple word a modest triumph in the rhythm of their restored everyday life.

The young manager hovered nearby, tablet clutched in nervous fingers, his unease radiating like heat shimmer off asphalt as he awaited the boss's arrival. "I heard that they couldn't find any of the snowmen."

Adam smiled, "Yeah half the world thinks it's all fake, the other half thinks it's a military cover up."

Charlie erupted into the room then, a vortex of commanding energy, acknowledging Adam with a crisp nod and a handshake that gripped like tempered steel. "Adam, sorry for the wait! Since your adventure, business has ten-fold." The manager passed over the tablet, its screen alive with schematics that pulsed like the blueprints of some grand, mechanical destiny. Charlie pored over them, his brow creasing in furrowed concentration, then shifted his gaze to the manager, and finally to Adam. "Are you sure about this?" he pressed, his tone laden with the gravity of fiscal asteroids. "It's going to be very costly. At least triple the cost of the first one."

Adam eased deeper into the yielding embrace of his chair, the teacup a familiar bulwark against the world's sharper edges. He savored another sip, the liquid's heat a defiant echo against the lingering phantom of glacial ice, and inclined his head in affirmation. His fingers danced across the tablet's surface, halting at the social media video feed where monetization credits cascaded in an unending stream, a veritable torrent of virtual aurum. "Oh yeah," Adam replied, his voice steady as bedrock, laced with unshakeable certainty. "Do it."

Charlie leaned forward, intrigue sparking in his eyes like ignited plasma. "Where are you planning on going with all these modifications?"

Adam paused, letting the query linger in the air like an unspoken equation waiting to be solved. "The earth," he murmured, "is a lot bigger than we were led to believe." With a fluid motion, he rotated the tablet toward Charlie, revealing images of colossal ice mountains that towered like the ramparts of forgotten worlds. "Beyond the ice wall," he declared, the phrase ringing with the resonance of revelation and vow. "I want to see what's out there."

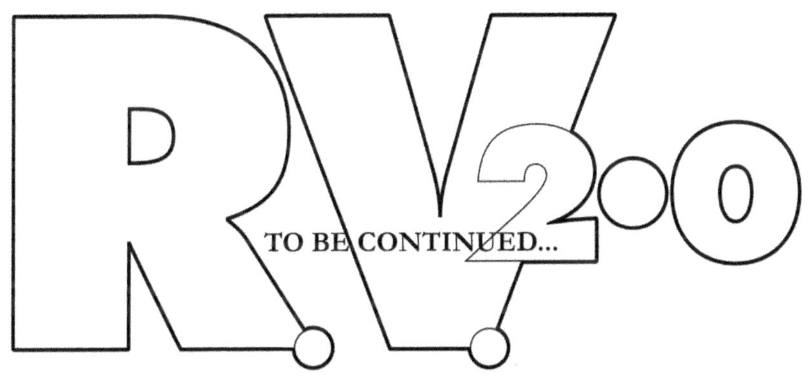

R.V. 2.0
TO BE CONTINUED...

CriticalBlast•com

Follow the early 1900s AB FROST Book Series re-imagined for todays audience.

EXCITING CHILDREN'S STORIES OF GRAND IMAGINATION TO EXPLORE!

We recommend these DEVILISH books be read with the lights on!

DISCOVER WHAT YOUR NEIGHBOURS ARE UP TO!